I0672078

Dragon Masters (Book 2 of the Eumetadotos Series)

Cover image: Pierre (artbypierre on Fiverr.)

Edited by: Amy Hertzog

ISBN: 978-0-9978449-2-4

ISBN-13: 978-0-9978449-3-1

DEDICATION

This book is dedicated to my daughters, Abigail and Cecilia. Our family may be little, and broken, but it's still good. Yep, still good. Always remember that we always have each other. I love you two so very, very much.

Dragon Masters (Book 2 of the Eumetadotos Series)

Prologue

Joshua lay in his bed, listening to the world around him. He grew more and more impatient as time went on. He could hear everyone talking around him, but couldn't respond. His body may have been rendered immobile, but his hearing was not affected in the slightest. It was infuriating to want to interject his valuable opinions in matters of battle, but was not able to move or communicate at all. His eyes were closed, so he couldn't even see what was happening around him, which irritated him even more.

He had heard what the Dark Figure had said to Arianna. He had heard his friends come in and help her fight it off. He felt helpless that he could not come to her aid. Instead, everyone was coming to his.

He sighed in his mind. He had made such a mess of his relationship with Arianna. Inside, he knew that he had to allow her to grow and to use her powers. He had heard the prophecy himself. She was destined to save the realm. He knew that she had to fulfill that destiny. However, it went against everything that he had been trained to do. His job was to protect the Royal Family. He had failed her parents. He didn't want to fail her too.

He loved her, but he feared her powers. Magic was never spoken of in Eumetadotos, except to talk about the evil, or the Elves. She was part Elf, one quarter, to be exact. How would that work? Would she be immortal? Would she adopt their prejudices against humans? She couldn't. She was three quarters human herself. She couldn't hate the majority of herself, could she? He doubted that Arianna could hate anyone.

He heard the door open and soft footsteps come in. He heard the sound of a chair being dragged next to the bed. Why she didn't just leave it there, he didn't know. A slight feeling of irritation came over him, but passed quickly. The woman with the soft voice was back. He knew that he knew her voice, but couldn't place her. The only voice that he knew under this accursed spell was Arianna's. He couldn't figure out why.

"Joshua, it's me again. Can you hear me?" A pause. "That's a stupid question to ask. I know you can't, or if you can, you can't respond." A sigh. "Help is on the way. I hope it is soon. I hate seeing you like this. I wish that I could do something more for you."

Joshua wanted to tell her that what she had been doing was more than enough. She kept him updated on the latest news and soothed him with her voice. He started to grow agitated with his condition again. He just wanted to see who it was that was speaking to him.

The woman began to sing quietly. He wanted to turn and see who was sitting with him. She came in often and informed him of what was happening while he was lying here, useless. She didn't think that he could hear her, but he could. He heard every word. Her voice was soothing. It almost made him relax and forget about the fact that he couldn't move. She stopped singing and started talking again.

"We still haven't heard from Arianna and the others. They've been gone almost a week with no word. We're all getting worried. Armen is talking about sending someone else over to find them. I don't know what is going to happen. I'm scared."

He wanted to reach out and touch her and tell her that it would be ok. The thought struck him as odd. He was in love with Arianna. The queen infuriated him with her stubbornness, and her strong will, but he loved her just the same. When she broke off the engagement, his heart had been broken.

"I guess the elf and I have something in common after all," he thought. "She broke both of our hearts."

The only difference between them is that Ellavorn was not under this curse. No, he was on Arianna's little quest to find that wizard. If he could have shaken his head, he would have. It was a fool's errand. Now, the four of them were stuck in another realm, looking for some person that they had never met, and probably never even seen. How did they know what to look for?

The woman's voice continued. He felt guilty about drowning her out. He decided to listen to her. She was reading aloud this time. A story of a girl who fell into a well while making a wish. It was a nice story. If he were ever to wake up from this accursed sleep, he would have to be sure to find her and ask her what the story was called. If he remembered it at all.

Her voice really was soft and beautiful. He listened to her tell the story and started to feel tired. She had that effect on him. She could always relax him to the point where he would actually fall asleep. He never heard her leave after her visits. Between the singing and the stories, she would lull him to sleep, like a child. He began to balk at that idea, but it was kind of comforting as well.

In his mind, he began to compare the woman who came to visit him and Arianna. Arianna's voice was strong. She was caring, yes, but she had more of a regal tone in her voice. She was not one to put up with any nonsense. This woman's voice was sweeter, softer, and gentler. He found himself looking forward to her visits. He just wished that he could place her voice. He knew that her voice was familiar. He just couldn't place it with a face. It was beginning to really bother him.

He didn't even remember everything about coming into the castle that day. He remembered the imposter who called himself Wyatt Redwood falling from the horse to his death, and then, blackness. He had heard Arianna's hysterical voice after the Dark Figure placed the curse on him. He had tried to respond, but he couldn't. He heard everyone burst into the room and the commotion that ensued. He felt himself being carried and placed on his bed. The irritation of the situation began to creep in again. He wanted to kill this thing. This thing that kept threatening his queen, his kingdom and who placed this curse on him.

The woman's voice broke through his thoughts. He began to feel tired. He knew that he would see her in his dreams, but would wake up and forget her face again. Another side effect of the curse, he assumed, as he drifted off into sleep, listening to her voice. That sweet, beautiful voice.

The woman stood up from her seat and closed the book of fairy tales, placing it on the dresser in Joshua's room. She replaced the chair and walked over to straighten the covers over him. She looked at him longingly and went to the door. She turned to give him one long, last look and slipped out as a tear slipped out of her eye and down her cheek. This was the hardest part of her day, leaving his side.

Chapter 1

As Arianna and Ellavorn stepped through the portal, they found themselves on a gorgeous river bank, surrounded by a forest. The trees were tall and dense so they could not see how far they went back. Adasser and Tanelia had split up and started walking towards the tree line to determine any dangers that they may find.

"Watch out!" Tanelia's scream rang out across the beach. Arianna threw her hands up and melted the spears that were flying towards them. They looked in Tanelia's direction and noticed that she had fallen to the ground. The other three began to run to her side to assess and injuries that she may have. Arianna and Ellavorn reached her first.

She sat up and flinched. There was a deep gash on her arm and blood was streaming down. Ellavorn knelt beside her and reached for her arm. He cradled it in his arm and held his hands against it. His hands began to glow and her skin stitched itself back up, good as new.

"Thank you," she half growled at him as she snatched her arm back out of his grasp.

"You're welcome, Tanelia," Ellavorn replied before standing and walking back to Arianna.

Adasser reached them and took one look at the situation and figured out what was going on. He shook his head and picked up one of the spears that Arianna hadn't melted with her powers.

"The crest of the wizard is burned into this." He pointed it out to the others. "This was surely set up as a first line of defense. This must be the correct path. Tanelia, are you alright? Can you handle the rest of this mission?"

Tanelia half groaned, half sighed. "I am fine, Adasser. Luckily, our prince is still an adequate healer."

"Adequate?"

"You will do."

"Tanelia, that is enough of this contempt," Ellavorn's voice grew strained. It was true; he and Tanelia had been together at one point. That was before he met Arianna. He had loved her, but something changed in him that day and he couldn't explain what. She hadn't taken the rejection well, and he could understand that. But, it had been years since that day and she still was acting out. He was growing tired of her disdain. Yes, they had been an item, but he was still her prince. He respected that she was hurt by his decision to end their relationship. He even respected that she would hate him; however, he grew tired of the lack of respect that she continuously showed for him.

"I know that I hurt you, but you must move on."

"Move on? The way you moved on? You left me for a

human!"

"I know and I will not apologize for that. I love Arianna. I feel badly that I hurt you, but I cannot apologize for the way that I feel about her. I did not choose to fall in love with her. No one chooses who they love. Love just happens, whether we expect it to or not. You have to move on and let go. You will be miserable if you don't."

"Who says I haven't moved on? Who says I am still in love with you, traitor?"

"I do not assume that you are still in love with me. However, only a fool would not be able to see that you are still holding on to the pain. And do not *ever* call me a traitor again. If you value your position in the royal court, you will show your prince the respect that he deserves."

"Deserves? You think that a human lover deserves respect? What are you going to do when she dies? What then, Ellavorn? Are you going to try and come back to the Glen and expect us to welcome you with open arms? What of your children? Will they rule Eumetadotos or will they become the heirs to the Elven throne? They would carry human blood inside of them. You're not just a traitor; you're a traitor of the worst kind. Not only are you tainting Elven blood, but you are tainting *Royal* Elven blood with mortality. No, I no longer love you. You disgust me."

Ellavorn's anger grew with every word that spewed from her mouth. Her hatred of humans did not surprise him in the least. It shamed him because he once shared those feelings as well. No, he was not surprised at her hatred of the human race. What he was surprised at was the ease that she felt spewing that hatred towards him. She was entitled to feel that way. He could not change the way that she felt. However, he expected her to act more civilized than she had been.

Tanelia had always been feisty. It was part of what attracted him to her in the first place. She had her ideals, and she stuck to them. However, she had always shown him respect, up until recently. He knew that she did not approve of his engagement to Arianna because of her bloodline, but she had never treated him with such scorn before. The lack of respect was beginning to infuriate him.

"Tanelia, I will tell you one last time. The lack of respect stops immediately. If you continue to act this way, I will have no choice but to relieve you of your position. You are acting borderline treasonous. Whether you agree with my decisions or not, I am still your prince, and I am in command, whether you like it or not. You will not make any more rude comments from here on out. Do I make myself clear?"

Tanelia sneered at him. "Crystal." She bowed and almost mockingly said, "Your Majesty."

Ellavorn turned to Adasser. "What do you feel is the best course of action?"

Adasser looked from Ellavorn to Tanelia and back. "We should start through those trees from where the spears came. They were most likely put there by the wizard's family to protect them. I assume that would be the best path to take."

Ellavorn nodded. "Lead the way."

Adasser nodded and started toward the tree line. As he passed Tanelia, he grabbed her arm and led her to the side.

"Please excuse me for one moment while I consult my second in command."

Adasser led Tanelia out of ear shot and Ellavorn and Arianna watched from afar.

"What do you think he's saying to her?" Arianna inquired.

"I don't know. Hopefully, he is enforcing what I told her about the lack of respect."

"You know that she is lying, don't you?"

"What is she lying about, Arianna?"

Arianna smiled. "She's still in love with you, Ellavorn."

"Why would you say that?"

"Because she is still hurting. If she wasn't in love with you, she wouldn't hurt so badly. She's lashing out because it hurts her to see you with me. She loves you, but you broke her heart. She may be a fierce warrior, but she still has feelings."

"Maybe you're right. I don't know what Tanelia feels. I know only that she holds contempt for humans, and because I am in love with a human, she hold contempt for me as well."

"What about Adasser?"

"Adasser holds no contempt for me."

"No, I mean, why doesn't she hate him? He not only fell in love with my grandmother, but had an affair and had a child with her."

Ellavorn smiled sadly. "Tanelia thinks of Adasser as a father figure. He has been her mentor for as long as I can remember. Her parents were not around much when she was growing up. They were sent on missions to other Elven domains and felt that she would be better off staying home. They knew that she was going to be a warrior, so they arranged for her to start training while they were away. Adasser took her in and practically raised her as his own.

"I am sure that she feels that he betrayed our lineage as well, but I cannot see her loathing him as she does me. In addition, he is not royalty, whereas I am. So, that complicates things a little more."

Arianna nodded. "Ellavorn, you speak as though we are still together."

"Wishful thinking, perhaps? I hope that we can discuss it at some point."

Arianna smiled. "I would definitely like to discuss that. Maybe after we save our realm from certain destruction?"

Ellavorn laughed. Adasser whistled to them and the four entered the forest to begin their search.

Chapter 2

The journey into the woods was silent at first. Adasser and Tanelia took the lead and Ellavorn and Arianna followed closely behind. They would stop here and there so that Adasser and Tanelia could listen and assess their surroundings, leading them in different directions. No one wanted to break the ice and be the first to speak. After walking for hours, Adasser stopped and turned to the group.

"We should stop and set up camp here. There is a stream just over there." He pointed in the direction. "We can fill our water supplies with that and continue our journey in the morning."

They began to prepare their site. Tanelia began casting a protection spell on the area to alert them if any visitors found them. Arianna and Ellavorn took the water containers to the stream and began to fill them. Adasser waved his hand and tents magically appeared for them to sleep in. He also grabbed a bow to hunt for food.

"I thought that Elves were not allowed to harm other living creatures or their immortality would be forfeit?" Arianna asked Ellavorn.

"We are allowed to hunt for food. We are not permitted to take a life for no good reason. If it is to sustain our health or in self-defense, then it is allowable. However, we cannot kill for sport."

Arianna nodded in understanding.

"Adasser is a very skilled hunter. He should be able to find something good to eat."

A little while later, a fire had been started and was ready for cooking. Adasser came walking back to camp with a deer and a few rabbits. The foursome cooked and ate their food in relative silence. Ellavorn was right. Adasser had done a great job of acquiring what they needed and more. There would be plenty of food for another few days if they needed it.

After dinner, they all moved to their tents to get some sleep. Arianna lay on the ground, tossing and turning, trying to fall asleep, but she just couldn't. She decided to go and sit in front of the fire and try to clear her thoughts. She got lost in her thoughts and didn't hear someone walking up. She just about jumped out of her skin when they cleared their throat.

"Oh, it's just you," she looked up at the contemptuous face that she had gotten used to seeing lately.

"What are you doing out of your tent? We don't know the dangers of this place. You could get yourself killed."

"What do you care? Isn't that what you want?"

Tanelia sighed and sat down hard on the ground across

from Arianna.

"You would think so, but I do not wish you dead, Your Highness."

Arianna gave her a distrustful look.

Tanelia sighed. "Honestly. I do not. I do not like you very much, but I do not wish death upon you."

"Well, that's a consolation," Arianna said sarcastically.

"What would you do were you in my position?"

"What position is that?"

"The man that I loved left me for a human, who at the time was a mere child! He left me for someone who will probably die and he is willing to taint his bloodline with mortality for her...for you. He shared my views until you came along. Now, I no longer know him. You stole that from me. How am I supposed to not dislike you?"

"I had no control over any of this. I never chose any of this. I will not apologize for loving him, Tanelia. I do love him still."

"You turned him away!"

"I was grieving! I had just lost both of my parents in one day! I was not thinking properly. I have regretted that decision every second since."

"You turned him away and yet he still came back to you."

"He was protecting me."

"He has to protect you because you are a helpless human."

"No, he was protecting me because that is what you do when you love someone. And I am not a mere human, am I? I do share part of your heritage. That is my grandfather there." She pointed to Adasser's tent.

"So, why do you not show the same contempt for Adasser that you show for Ellavorn?"

Tanelia looked away. "I have my reasons."

"Ellavorn said that you think of him as a father figure. That he practically raised you."

She nodded, wordlessly.

"He loved my grandmother."

"Yes, I heard."

"He fell in love and had a child with a human, yet, you do not display the same contempt for him that you do for Ellavorn."

"No, I do not. Adasser is also not royalty."

"I think that you are still in love with Ellavorn."

Tanelia scoffed. "Why would you think that?"

"Because you're still hurting."

"Who said that I'm hurting?"

"Your eyes."

"Oh, so now you've become an expert on my eyes?"

"No. But, I do see the way that you look at him."

Tanelia rolled her eyes. "And how do I look at him?"

"Like you lost the love of your life."

Tanelia looked away and stayed silent.

"I am sorry that you are hurting. I truly am. I know that you hate humans because we are mortal. I can't change your view on that, nor will I try to. Your feelings are your own. But, just know this. Not all humans are bad. Yes, we die, but so do some elves from what I hear." Tanelia flinched. "Mortality does not define us. As far as I know, Elves are the only species that is immortal. Do you also hate the other creatures? You seem to care for animals very much. So, why hold such contempt for humans alone?"

"Humans are reckless. They are violent. Just look at Iron Demon. He is vengeful and prideful and just despicable."

"That is true about some. But, most humans are good. It is all in the way that you choose to look at us. Yes, there are wars and conflict. But, the good far outweighs the bad. Not all humans are like Iron Demon. I agree with you that he is a despicable example of a human being. But, not all of us are like him, Tanelia."

Tanelia looked at Arianna, deep in thought.

"Maybe not, but the fact remains that your kind dies."

"Have you again forgotten that I am, apparently, one of a kind? We don't know if I die yet."

Tanelia rolled her eyes. "Your Majesty, I believe that it is truly time to go to bed now. Please go back to your tent so that I may return to mine."

Arianna smiled, knowing that she had, on some level, gotten the best of the sharp-tongued elf. She stood and went back to her tent. When she got there, she turned to look back at Tanelia, still sitting by the fire. She felt a stab of pity for her for a moment. Tanelia may be tough and hard to get along with, but Arianna felt that there was more to her than could be seen on the surface. She may never be friends with the elf, but she was going to try to at least get her to see that humans aren't so bad after all.

Chapter 3

The next morning, Arianna emerged from her tent and found Tanelia and Adasser standing by the fire, cooking some of the rabbit meat that Adasser had caught the night before and discussing the plan for the day.

Adasser smiled when he saw her. "Good morning, Arianna. I hope that you slept well?" He guided her over to a log and both sat down.

Arianna nodded. "Yes, thank you." She looked at Tanelia, who dropped her eyes to the fire. Neither one said anything more, but some of the tension that had been stewing between them had eased just a little.

Just then, Ellavorn emerged from his tent, looking disheveled. Arianna tried to hide her amusement, but a small smile escaped her lips. She had never seen him look anything but perfectly put together.

"Can we finish this quest so that I no longer have to sleep on the ground," Ellavorn grumbled as he pulled a leaf from his hair.

Adasser leaned over to Arianna and whispered, "Our prince does *not* find pleasure in the early morning hours." Arianna giggled.

Ellavorn heard the exchange and shot them a withering look. It had the opposite effect that he had hoped for, as they both started laughing.

Tanelia let out a huff. "How can you be laughing when we have a mission to complete? This is of the utmost importance! We do not have time for the two of you to be making jokes."

Adasser stood and put his hand on her shoulder. "Tanelia, even in the darkest of times, you still have to look for light and laughter. Otherwise, the darkness will consume you."

She turned to look at Adasser and shook her head.

"We don't have the time for this. We need to find that wizard and convince him to return to Eumetadotos as soon as we can. That Dark Figure will not waste time taking over the kingdom if it figures out that we are gone!"

"The kingdom is safe. We got the people out. That figure is no match for Armen. Otherwise, he would have attacked the Glen as well."

"We don't know that. Maybe he was going for the easier targets first," she waved her arm in Arianna's direction. "She may be part Elf, but she still does not understand the extent of her powers. She didn't even know that she had them until recently. Not to mention the fact that she is cursed!"

"Was cursed. Have you so quickly forgotten her sacrifice?"

"No, I have not." She wheeled around on Arianna. "How could you have been so careless with your kingdom? Iron Demon is now king! How are you going to force him to abdicate the throne back to you?"

Arianna looked at her with no emotion on her face. "I have a plan for that."

Tanelia rolled her eyes and sat across from Arianna. "How are you going to get the most vile, evil human I have ever come across to listen to you?"

Arianna let a small smile escape. "Well, he has no choice, now does he? He is locked in the dungeon. His freedom hinges on his willingness to abdicate. Only a select few know that I actually abdicated my throne to him. If he refuses, I can still rule my kingdom and he can rot in that cell."

Tanelia looked away, a glimmer of a smile starting to spread across her lips.

"Well, Your Majesty. It seems I just may have underestimated you after all." She stood and walked away.

Ellavorn witnessed the exchange and walked over and sat down. He glanced at Arianna with a look of amusement on his face.

"Melting the heart of ice, are you?"

Arianna looked at him, startled. "What do you mean?"

He raised his eyebrows. "Tanelia. I saw her smile before she walked away."

"Oh. Yes. I guess she thinks that my plan is a good one."

"It was a risk that you took, Arianna. A big risk."

"I know. I had to take that risk. My kingdom is at stake. I could not risk coming here with that curse still on me and running out of the elixir. I had to do something. It was the only thing that I could think of."

"You know that Iron Demon is not going to give up that position easily."

"I figured as much. But, I will prevail. He will abdicate his position or he will die in that cell."

"And what will happen then?"

"He has no next of kin, am I correct?"

"None that are known. He is too feared for women to find attractive. He has no other family."

"The throne will then pass back to me, as my family has

ruled for centuries and my bloodline is that of the rightful rulers of Eumetadotos. I do not wish for him to die, but I cannot subject my people to his insanity."

Ellavorn smiled at her and said, "Once again, you amaze me with how much you have grown. You are not thinking of yourself, but of your people."

"That is what a queen is supposed to do."

"Yes, I know. But, far too many do not take that into consideration. They allow the power to get the better of them and they forget that they are supposed to think of the well-being of their kingdom, and not of themselves. To be a leader requires selflessness. Unfortunately, it is a natural tendency to become power hungry and put your own wishes ahead of everyone else's."

Arianna smiled a sad smile as she let those words sink in as Adasser approached with the cooked meat for breakfast. Once their food had been eaten, they began to pack up the camp to continue their journey.

Adasser and Tanelia led the group, ever alert for signs that Arianna couldn't see, or was not aware of.

"How do they know that we are on the correct path?"

Ellavorn smiled and said, "Our warrior elves are trained quite well in many different aspects, including tracking. They look for signs that you and I would not know to look for.

Adasser and Tanelia are the best at what they do. It is the reason that they hold the highest ranks. They have to be seeing some sort of sign that we are on the right track."

Suddenly, Adasser and Tanelia stopped short. They both held up their hands, signaling Arianna and Ellavorn to catch up. They exchanged a glance that spoke volumes between them and both of them whipped out weapons from seemingly nowhere.

Arianna stood in stunned silence, wondering what was going on.

"Ellavorn, get Arianna and yourself up into a tree where you will be safe. We will hold them off," said Tanelia, her tone was eerily steady.

"Who," Arianna inquired.

"Wolves," came her reply.

"Arianna, come quickly, up this tree," said Ellavorn.

"I want to help, Ellavorn."

"Arianna, this is no time to argue, get up in that tree now. That is a direct order," Adasser's voice was full of irritation.

Arianna hadn't heard that tone in his voice before, so she begrudgingly went with Ellavorn as he helped her up into the tree.

They found a sturdy branch and settled in to watch the fight.

"I don't understand why we can't help fight them off."

"Arianna, have you ever seen a real wolf?"

"Well, no."

"Watch."

Arianna turned herself so that she could see Adasser and Tanelia. They stood stock still and ready to attack at a moment's notice. She observed how their bodies were tighter than bowstrings, steady and strong. They made no movements. Not even the slightest flinch.

"What are they doing? They're like sitting ducks."

"Watch. They are tracking them, making ready for the attack. From how it looks, there are a few wolves in the pack."

"How can you tell?"

"I've seen them do this before. I told you, they are the best at what they do. Trust them."

Arianna heard a rustling sound coming from the left of the two warriors. They kept steady until an enormous wolf, at least four feet tall on all fours, leapt from behind a bush, aiming for the two of them. In one fluid motion, both of them turned and fired off arrows, aiming for the wolf's heart and hitting their target. The wolf fell dead at their feet. Arianna gasped at the scene that had just unfolded before her.

She had never seen movement so beautiful, yet so deadly at the same time. She gained a newfound respect for both of the warriors in that moment. As she was taking it all in, six more wolves, all around the same size as the first, appeared. She looked at Ellavorn in a panic. He did not seem fazed. They watched, quietly from their perch as they felled five of the wolves. The sixth had disappeared from sight. Adasser and Tanelia started to search for it, but to no avail.

Adasser looked up to find Arianna and Ellavorn's position. His eyes grew wide in fear. Arianna followed his gaze, to find a snarling wolf in the tree next to theirs, looking at them, in an attack position. She grew stiff with fear, and swallowed hard. Adasser and Tanelia were in no position to attack the wolf without the risk of hurting Ellavorn or Arianna.

Arianna looked at Ellavorn, and his face wore the same mask of fear and disbelief as hers. That was enough to spur her into action. She set her face in a look of determination and turned quickly, throwing her hands up, igniting a huge ball of light from them, launching it directly at the wolf as it began its leap towards them. The light hit it squarely in the chest, forcing an ear-splitting yelp, and the mongrel fell to the ground with a sickening crunch.

Ellavorn and Arianna looked down from their position, to see the body of the wolf, twisted in unnatural positions. Arianna looked at Ellavorn, who was looking at her with an expression of mixed shock, disbelief and pride. She looked back down at the wolf and tears began to form.

"Arianna, you did what you had to do to protect us. That wolf would have surely killed us if you hadn't done that. How *did* you do that?"

"I don't know. It just happens."

"I have never seen anything like it. That was truly amazing."

They climbed down from their perch as Adasser and Tanelia came walking over. Adasser grabbed Arianna into a huge hug.

"That was truly remarkable."

She pulled herself away to look at the wolf that she had killed up close. She turned around, but it was gone. She whipped her head back to the others.

"Where did it go?"

They all looked around. All of the bodies of the wolves that had just been littering the forest floor had disappeared without a trace.

Adasser and Tanelia settled back into their position, trying to track anything else, but nothing was there.

"This must be the work of the wizards. They are masters of illusions," Adasser tried to come up with an explanation.

"So, the wolves were not real," Arianna sounded incredulous at the idea.

"Oh, they were very real, in a manner of speaking."

"Explain."

"Those wolves were obviously another form of protection for the wizards. They were put there to try to stop someone from approaching any further. They could inflict damage on someone; however, they are not true wolves. They are illusions, but deadly ones. It would explain the lack of blood that Tanelia and I noticed when we shot the first one."

"What do you mean?"

"When the wolf landed, we saw our arrows, but there was no blood. Normally, there would be. With this kill, there was nothing."

Arianna shuddered at the thought of how many kills that Adasser had under his belt. He was quite old, and he had been commander for a very long time.

"I have fought the wizard's illusions before. When I began

my training, it was protocol for the wizard to produce them for us to fight off. It was the perfect technique. He would conjure some pretty hideous beasts and we would fight them off. It was a controlled area, where he could call them off before they could inflict any harm, and they *could* inflict harm."

Adasser held out his left arm, and for the first time, Arianna noticed a jagged two scars, distanced enough to have been made by wolf fangs, running from his mid-bicep to just below his elbow.

"We were fighting wolves, much like these. I took my eyes off of him for a split second. He bit me, and once his teeth had torn my flesh, he dragged his teeth down my arm until I was able to put a dagger between his eyes."

Ellavorn moved forward to look at the scar.

"Why did you not let someone heal it?"

"I did, but only to a point. I want that scar to stay there. It reminds me to never take my eye off of the main goal. I did once and it almost cost me my life. It is a reminder to be ever vigilant."

Adasser turned to Arianna. "Be ever vigilant, Arianna. Do not allow anyone or anything distract you from anything important. Sometimes, there are no second chances in life."

Arianna nodded in understanding.

"Now, let's continue on our way."

Chapter 4

The group sat for a few moments to gather their strength and to rest. They began to move again, following Tanelia and Adasser, stopping only to eat again. They traveled until the sun began to set and decided to set up camp again. Tanelia again set up protection spells and the rest set up camp. After they ate, they all returned to their tents to sleep.

As Arianna lay in her tent, she could not seem to fall asleep. Her thoughts kept wandering back to Eumetadotos and Abigail and Joshua and the rest of her friends. She could not help but think of Joshua, laying in his bed and not being able to wake up. She felt guilty about leaving poor Abigail in charge while she was on this journey. She wondered how she was holding things together. She also wondered about Charlie, and his youthful eagerness to help. Her thoughts kept racing, and she could not find sleep, so she wandered out to the fire and sat down, staring into the flames.

She was so lost in her thoughts that she did not notice Ellavorn come out and sit next to her. She startled and smiled at him.

"Having a hard time falling asleep?"

"Yes," she said with a sigh. "I am missing my friends and worried about them. Joshua is under that sleeping curse. I don't know how to wake him. I was told that the only way was to either defeat the Dark Figure or..."

"Or what?"

"Or to ask you to wake him."

"Oh."

"Ellavorn, Joshua and I are no longer engaged."

"I know."

"I do not wish to ask you any favors. There has to be another way."

"Arianna, I will wake him when we return."

Arianna's head whipped round to study his profile, as he kept his face straight ahead.

"I know that you love him. I would do anything to make you happy." He turned to look at her. "Including awaken Captain Oakford from that curse. It would be the more humane thing to do anyway. Sleeping curses are horrible. You are aware of everything around you, yet, you can do nothing to help."

"You speak as though you have been under one."

"Not personally. I know a few elves that have been. I have some experience in breaking sleeping curses. Those who have been under them have shared their experiences with me, and others."

"You would awaken Joshua for me?"

"I would. As I said, I would do anything for you. I love you, Arianna. I always will."

"I love you as well; you know that, don't you?"

Ellavorn smiled in response. "You sent your army out to find me. How could I not know that? I was hit over the head with that brick a long time ago."

Arianna laughed at their shared joke. It seemed as though a decade had passed since that day in the Forest Glen.

"I still love you too, Ellavorn."

Ellavorn smiled.

"Joshua and I are no longer engaged."

"You mentioned that. But, neither are we."

"I know. I'm sorry that I took my anger and grief out on you. I have regretted my decision every second since."

"You sent your guards out looking for me."

"I went to the Forest Glen looking for you first."

"You could have been killed! My father was furious when you broke our engagement and sent me away."

"I didn't know at first how my actions affected him. He listened to me and then sent me away, warning me about the consequences."

"It is why I gave you the koutí profiteíavoun. So that you could make amends."

"I know. I am eternally grateful for that. I don't know that we would have been able to put our differences aside if it weren't for that."

Ellavorn smiled. "I think that you would have found a way. You are quite intelligent and are proving time and time again that you are a problem solver. You would have figured something out without my help. I just found something to give my father a nudge in the right direction."

"How do you mean?"

"By reminding him of who you are."

Arianna looked at him, confused.

"Did you not listen to the prophecy?"

"Well, yes, but I don't understand what that has to do with his forgiveness."

"Arianna, we elves have known of the prophecy for centuries. It is one of our fairy tales that we were told as children. When you were born and word got out about the color of your eyes, we knew that the prophecy was going to be fulfilled through you. He was angry with you and he foolishly called off the alliance between our kingdoms. He acted out of hurt and anger and needed to be reminded of who you actually are. I sent the koutí profiteíavoun as a reminder for him."

"Well, again, I am grateful that you did and I am truly sorry for my actions."

"Arianna, I know that we are not in a place to make a decision about us, but I have to know what your intentions are when this is all over and we are victorious."

Arianna looked uncomfortable. "You mean if we are victorious. Ellavorn, we don't know what the future holds. I don't know if I can do this. I know that I have many behind me. However, this is resting on my shoulders. Tanelia is right. I just discovered my powers. I have no idea what I am capable of doing. I can train and I can hone my powers as best as I can, but will it be enough when the time comes for the final battle between the Dark Figure and myself?"

A voice from behind startled them both. "You have demonstrated more bravery in the short time that I have known you than some elves have shown in their entire lives."

Both of them turned to see Tanelia leaning against a tree, looking at them. Both looked at her with surprise and shock. She smirked at their faces and walked over and knelt in front of Arianna.

"Yes, I gave you a compliment. Arianna, I will not lie. I hated you when Ellavorn decided to leave me for you. I despised you when he announced his intentions to marry you. I was disgusted when they asked me to take this journey and protect you. However, I have been watching you, more than you know. You carry yourself with the dignity of a true queen. You are kind, generous and sincere. You have proven me wrong time and time again. Whether out of spite or because that is just who you are, I don't know, but it is quite impressive.

"I have seen you perform acts of bravery that I never imagined you were capable of. You have faced pure evil in multiple forms, you have made hard decisions, and you even killed a wolf today. You have proven that you are worthy of the prophecy. Your powers will grow, it is true. None of us know how much our powers will grow at any given time. Do not fear that. You are destined to do great things. Do not doubt yourself. You shall prevail."

Tanelia stood, patted Arianna's shoulder and walked back to her tent, closing the flap behind her.

Arianna and Ellavorn exchanged a shocked stare.

"Did that really just happen or am I dreaming," Arianna

whispered.

"No, that really happened."

Arianna smiled.

"Don't think that this means that we're friends," yelled Tanelia from her tent.

Arianna and Ellavorn began to laugh.

Chapter 5

The following morning dawned bright and sunny again. Arianna turned on her side from her back and groaned. Sleeping on the hard ground was beginning to bother her back. She wasn't used to not sleeping in her bed. She pushed herself up into a sitting position and sat for a moment before standing and leaving the tent.

The rest of the group were sitting around the fire, discussing the day's plan.

"Oh, I see you've decided to join us," Tanelia remarked, but with a tad less vinegar in her voice.

"I'm sorry. I didn't mean to sleep so late. I wish someone would have woken me."

Tanelia snorted. "I'm not your alarm clock."

Adasser sighed. "Tanelia, that is quite enough. I thought you were through with this childishness."

Tanelia rolled her eyes and indicated a plate of food for Arianna.

"Eat and get ready to go. We still have plenty of daylight to burn."

Arianna sat and picked up her plate. She ate her food quickly and busied herself helping break down the camp again. Adasser approached her with a smile.

"Tanelia is softening her stance on you."

"I feel like it's one step forward, two steps back with her. It seems as though as soon as I do something that she approves of, I do something that angers her in some way. I honestly did not mean to sleep that long."

Adasser laughed. "You didn't sleep much longer than Ellavorn did."

Arianna looked incredulous. "What? You mean to tell me that she was making me feel bad and I wasn't even holding us up that long?"

Adasser laughed. "I told you she was softening her stance on you."

Arianna looked confused, which made Adasser laugh even harder. "Tanelia is very strong-willed. She does not like to seem soft. However, if you know what to look for, you can see through the façade. She does not hate you any longer, Arianna. She is actually growing fond of you. Your indomitable spirit is admirable to an elf, especially one as proud as Tanelia. She is growing to respect you."

"I hope so. She is not someone that I would want to consider me an enemy."

Adasser nodded in agreement. "No, she is not. She makes for a very formidable enemy; that is certain."

"Ellavorn said that you practically raised her."

Adasser smiled and indicated to a log for them to sit down. "Yes. Her parents were not around much. She was born to be a warrior. I took her in and took care of her while she was training. She is the closest I have to a child that I raised myself."

He looked at Arianna and smiled. She nodded.

"I wish I had known you all my life."

"And I, you. However, we cannot change the past. We can only look to the future and see what it brings us. I will be glad to be in your life from here forward, if you will allow it."

Arianna beamed. "I would appreciate that immensely. I no longer have any living blood relatives. It would be nice to have at least one."

Adasser's smiled dipped a little. "I am sorry that your family is no longer alive. I cannot imagine the pain that you must be feeling."

"Thank you. I miss them every day, especially my mother. She always knew what to do and what to say. I don't know how to do this without her."

Adasser put his hand on her shoulder. "I did not know your mother, but I knew your grandmother. She was the same way. To lose someone of that caliber is heart wrenching. I have seen your character, Arianna. You would make them both proud. You are strong and kind and brave. I have no doubt that you are our greatest hope in this war."

"That is what scares me the most. How can I defeat this thing when I have only just discovered my heritage and my powers recently? I have not had the years of training that you and Tanelia have had. This is a huge burden to have on one's shoulders. I am not sure that I can do this."

Adasser gave her a reassuring smile. "And that is why I have faith in you. You are unlike so many others. You are quite powerful, Arianna, yet, you do not allow that power to control you. You stay humble. Power can be an addicting thing. Magic alone can be addicting. Yet, you have shown no signs of either of them changing your character. This is how I know that you are an asset, not a liability. Someone could be the most powerful being that has ever lived, yet, if their heart is unkind, they have nothing of importance. Greed is the biggest liability one can possess. It will always be someone's downfall.

"Take Iron Demon, for example. He excitedly took the title of king from you and look what happened. He is rotting in a cell, fighting for his life. If he had not been so quick to jump at the promise of riches and wealth, he would not be in his current situation."

Arianna let his words sink in. It made sense to her when she thought about it, but her fears were not fully assuaged. She knew that she still had a lot of growing to do and not much time to do it in.

Adasser, seemingly reading her thoughts, spoke up. "You have many people on your side to help you along the way. Do not doubt our loyalty to you, even Tanelia. We are all firmly on your side."

"Thank you. I just hope that I don't let you all down."

"I have faith in you that you won't. You have a lot of people behind you that are willing to lay down their lives for you in order to help you."

"But the prophecy says that I will deliver the realm from evil. I don't know if I can do that on my own."

"The prophecy says that you will deliver, yes, but it does not say how. You are in charge here, Arianna. You are leading us. The prophecy does not state that you must act alone. It simply states that you are a means to the end. Besides, a prophecy is just a prediction. It is not set in stone.

"Saving an entire realm is too much of a burden to put on one person. Focus on defeating the Dark Figure. If you broaden your focus on too many things at once, you will lose focus on what is important. The Dark Figure is the key to this war. It is what started everything. Focus on defeating it and leave the rest to us."

Adasser's talk seemed to raise Arianna's spirits. She still felt a weight on her shoulders, but it was significantly lightened by his words. She had been feeling a huge pressure since she heard the prophecy. Saving an entire realm was overwhelming. Adasser was right. If she didn't think of it as a whole, and just focus on defeating the Dark Figure, it did make it seem more feasible. She smiled and stood up.

"Well, I guess we better get moving so that I can make the Dark Figure face its doom. Which way are we heading today?"

Adasser stood and chuckled and pointed west.

Chapter 6

The group started walking with Tanelia and Adasser in the lead. Ellavorn and Arianna followed behind them, all of them poised and ready for any dangers that may lie ahead. Soon, they heard the sound of water running.

"It sounds as though there is water close by. We should fill our water supply," Tanelia said.

Adasser agreed and they followed the sound to a stream in the woods. They started to fill their water supply when something shimmering caught Arianna's eye a few feet away by the water's edge. She cautiously walked over to see what was making the beautiful colors. It looked like a scale of some sort. It was a brilliant, ruby color, but when the sun hit it just so, it looked as if were bursting into flames. It was warm, but not unpleasant, to the touch. She picked it up and carried it back to the group.

"What could this be?"

She showed her find to Adasser, who grew pale. Tanelia came up beside him and had the same reaction. Her hands made a move towards her swords. Their reactions made Arianna scared.

"It cannot be! It was slain!" Adasser's voice was a mixture of fear, awe and confusion.

"I helped slay it myself," Tanelia's voice echoed the same

mixture, "It was the last one! This is impossible."

Arianna looked between the two elves, waiting for an explanation. Ellavorn was the last to join them. He came up beside Arianna and his face paled as well.

"Is that…is that…a dragon's scale?"

Arianna looked from one elf to another, the fear finally making sense to her, and creeping into her as well."

Adasser was the first to speak. "We do not know for sure if it came from an actual dragon or if it was a scale plucked from the last one so many years ago."

"Adasser, do not be foolish. You know that a dragon's scale cannot survive for this long. The power would have faded when the dragon died. That dragon was slain long before the wizard even left the realm. We helped slay it!"

"What other explanation do we have, Tanelia? It is a dragon scale! The only other explanation would be that the wizard somehow had a dragon's egg that he took with him, and we made sure to eliminate all of the eggs in the realm after the dragon was slain."

"Wait…you did what?" Arianna could not believe that they would wipe out an entire species of creatures.

"Arianna, you do not understand the destruction that a

single dragon can do. They could level Eumetadotos in a single step. Not to mention if they let fire loose. One dragon could level five kingdoms in one fell swoop. They are extremely dangerous creatures. It was for our safety that we had to eliminate them."

Arianna understood their concern, but still was uneasy about their actions. She was also uneasy because she realized that she was growing steadily warmer and warmer. She looked around and noticed that her friends seemed to be feeling the say way. Tanelia and Adasser looked at each other, mirroring a look of sheer terror in each other's faces. That was when they heard the rustling noises coming from the west of their group. Arianna and Ellavorn froze. Tanelia drew her swords with lightning speed. Adasser drew his bow just as quickly.

"Ellavorn, Arianna, I would tell you to hide, but there is nowhere to hide against this foe. We will also need all of the help that you can give us against it. Do not allow your fear to get in the way. Ellavorn, you are not a warrior, so try to lay low in cases of injuries. Neither of you have ever seen a dragon, so try to prepare for what is coming through those trees."

Arianna and Ellavorn both nodded ascent and stood next to Adasser and Tanelia, trembling but ready to fight. Neither was prepared for the sight of the dragon that came through the trees, and it seemed as though Adasser and Tanelia were caught off guard too.

The dragon that came through the trees was enormous, about 30 feet tall. It looked nothing like the ugly dragons that Adasser and Tanelia had seen in the past, ones that Arianna and Ellavorn had merely heard stories of. This one was beautiful. Its scales were the color of rubies, glimmering in the sun. It was a sight to behold. Its head lowered, seemingly to inspect the foreigners on his land.

Tanelia and Adasser got into their fighting stances. The dragon seemed to sense the hostility and something in its eyes changed to match the vitriol being aimed at it. It spread its wings to the fullest wingspan, which was about 40 feet wide, taking down a few trees with this action. Its throat started to glow a deep yellow color.

"Run!" Adasser shouted.

The four of them scattered. Adasser shot an arrow at the dragon, narrowly missing his mark because the beast pulled its head back at the last moment. It shot a flame in Adasser's direction, missing him as he rolled out of the way.

Arianna saw that the dragon was going for Adasser and threw her hands up, a giant ball of light emanating from her hands, hitting the dragon on his right front flank.

The dragon roared and turned to find her. It threw a flame in her direction. She ducked and rolled away from it, narrowly escaping being burned.

Tanelia saw her chance to take a turn to fight. She had traded her swords for her bow and let three loose at once. One found its target right under the dragon's left wing. The other two fell to the ground. The dragon threw another flame in her direction.

Arianna threw another ball of light at it, hitting it in its hind quarters. The dragon and Arianna and her friends continued the attacks back and forth for over an hour, with no signs of the dragon tiring. Finally, Tanelia shot an arrow straight into the dragon's chest, missing its heart, but hitting where it made the dragon angry.

The dragon raised itself up on its hind legs in pain and anger, letting out a shriek as it did.

Arianna saw the chance and threw another ball of light, even larger than the last one, at it, striking it in the chest, and bringing it down on its back. It hit its head hard on the rocks and was knocked out cold.

Tanelia saw her chance and leaped up with her swords drawn, ready to slay the dragon.

"Stop!" yelled Arianna. "What are you doing?"

Tanelia looked at her, shocked. "I am going to cut its head off. Did you not see it nearly tried to kill us?"

"It poses no harm to us right now. Leave it. We can get out of here before it wakes up. It won't know where we went."

Adasser came over to Arianna. "Tanelia is right. Dragons have an extraordinary sense of smell. It will find us and pursue us. If we do not kill it now, it will put not only our lives in danger, but also the lives of anyone we come across as well. They are vengeful creatures. They will not give up until it kills us."

Arianna's eyes filled with tears and she turned to walk away so that she didn't have to see the sight when a ball of pink light came from the trees, hitting Tanelia and knocking her off the dragon to the ground.

"Arianna! What are you thinking?"

Arianna turned and observed the scene before her.

"I didn't do that!"

"Really?" Snarled Tanelia, "Then who did?"

"I did!" A voice from the direction from which the dragon had come rang out.

"You were going to kill my dragon!"

A girl of about 16 years old stepped out, her raven black hair falling in a straight curtain down her back. Her ice blue eyes were glistening with anger. Arianna thought that she looked familiar, but couldn't quite put her finger on where she knew her from.

"Your dragon attacked us!" Tanelia shot back.

"Roumpini would not do that without being provoked. He's gentle and sweet."

Tanelia and Adasser looked at each other with incredulous looks.

"Dragons are *not* gentle nor are they sweet," Tanelia fired off.

The girl looked at them her as though she had two heads. "I don't know what kind of dragons you have come across in your lifetime, but my dragons are gentle. They wouldn't dream of hurting anything unless they are provoked. So, what did you do to him?"

Adasser stepped forward. "I beg your pardon, but who are you?"

"I should ask you that question. You are in my territory."

He nodded, "I am Adasser, Protector of the Forest Glen. This is Tanelia, my second in command. This is Arianna, Queen of Eumetadotos, and over there, is Prince Ellavorn of the Forest Glen."

The girl's eyes grew wide and held a hint of fear or contempt, Arianna couldn't determine which.

"You aren't from this realm."

Arianna spoke up. "No, we have come to try to find the wizard. We desperately need his help."

The girl looked at Arianna. "Are you an elf too? I thought that they didn't associate themselves with humans."

"That is a complicated situation."

The girl looked suspicious of the group, but moved to Arianna and put her hand out to shake hands. Arianna looked at her hand, confused as to what to do. The girl noticed her confusion and smiled and pointed to Arianna's hand. Arianna put her hand out and the girl took it and shook it.

"You really are royalty. Don't even know how to shake hands. My name is Cecilia. The wizard that your family banished was my great-grandfather."

Arianna realized that she had seen the girl before, in the vision that Armen conjured of the wizard's relatives. She looked Cecilia in the eyes. "I am sorry. I understand that my ancestors acted irrationally."

Cecilia chuckled and waved her hand dismissively. "No worries. It was a long time ago. I wasn't around then. I have a good life here. I don't know much else about life there. Now, about my dragon."

Arianna turned to look at Ellavorn. "Do you think that your healing magic will work on a dragon?"

Ellavorn looked lost. "I have no idea. I've never seen one to try."

Cecilia spied him suspiciously. "Never mind. I will try it myself."

"Cecilia, Ellavorn is the best healer in the Forest Glen."

"Yes, Your Majesty, but he is still an *elf*." She spat the word elf out in disgust, mirroring the contempt oozed by Tanelia when she spoke about humans. This was not lost on anyone in the group.

As Cecilia climbed up on the dragon, whom she had called Roumpini, she noticed the arrow by his wing. She scrunched her face up in irritation and left it there for the time being, shooting daggers at Tanelia and Adasser. She huffed and made her way to his head and began stroking his nose and singing a low, sweet song to him that Arianna recognized from her childhood. Cecilia was singing a lullaby to the dragon like a mother would to a child.

Roumpini's eyes began to open and his mouth seemed to turn into a smile. Cecilia climbed down and he got to his feet. She stood in front of him and pointed to the arrow.

"Sorry, boy. I have to keep that there until we get home."

The dragon seemed to nod as though he understood her. He then noticed that the group was still there. In one fell swoop, he grabbed Cecilia in his front claws and wrapped his wings around them both, and peeked over the top, seemingly to protect them from any further attacks from the group and to keep an eye on them.

"Roumpini, it's ok. They're not going to hurt you anymore. I won't let them. They're from the other realm. The one that grandfather told us about."

Roumpini seemed to understand every word that Cecilia told him and looked at the group in a kind of awe and wonder. He set Cecilia down on the ground and nuzzled her. She reached up and patted his nose and smiled.

"Good boy. Roumpini, this is Arianna, she's a queen, Ellavorn, and he's a prince, Adasser and Tanelia. They are protectors. They are all elves...well, three of them are."

Roumpini looked at them all with what seemed to be excitement. Adasser and Tanelia looked at each other in confusion. They had never seen a dragon act this way before. This dragon, aside from being beautiful, was, indeed, gentle and sweet, almost like a puppy.

Adasser addressed Cecilia first, "How can this be? Dragons are ruthless creatures. They destroy without blinking.

They do not typically understand what anyone is saying to them. How is this possible?"

Cecilia smiled. "Magic does not only exist in your realm, Adasser."

Adasser nodded, confused.

"You will understand in time. Come, I will guide you the rest of the way to my family's home."

The group followed Cecilia and Roumpini through the woods, still bewildered by the turn of events that had just occurred.

Chapter 7

As the group made their way to Cecilia's home, Arianna made her way up the line to speak to her more.

"I am sorry that we attacked your dragon. We didn't know that he was friendly. The only dragons that Adasser and Tanelia have ever encountered were dangerous. Ellavorn and I have never seen one before. We were in a defensive stance and I guess Roumpini thought we were going to attack."

"It's ok. I get it. He really is a big sweetheart."

"I see that now."

Roumpini lowered his massive head and Arianna stroked it, marveling at how smooth his scales felt under her fingertips. They felt like smooth, polished rubies. He was, indeed, a beautiful sight to behold.

"I thought that dragons were extinct? They no longer exist in our realm. They were long gone before...well, you know the incident."

Cecilia smiled. "Your Majesty – "

"Arianna, please."

Cecilia blinked, "Right. Arianna, you don't have to be embarrassed or ashamed of the past. You did not make those decisions nor did you do what your ancestors did. You do not seem to be frightened by magic, as you seem to possess it yourself. Our families did have a conflict in the past, but I do not hold it against you. Please do not try to erase history. To erase history erases the lessons we've learned from it."

Arianna smiled. "You're right. I hope that we can make a fresh start from here out."

Cecilia grinned. "I think that I would like that with you," she shot a furtive look back at the Elves, "I am not so sure about them, though."

Arianna looked confused. "Why?"

"Elves are immortal. That isn't natural. It goes directly against all laws of nature. Everything must die. It is the circle of life. To go on forever, it is just not natural. It disrupts that circle."

"I guess I never really thought about it that way. I know in our realm, a lot of the Elves do not like humans because of our mortality. They view it as a weakness."

Cecilia huffed. "To live your life sure that you have another day to live, that, to me, is weakness. To face mortality every day and know that today could be your last that is a sign of strength."

"I can understand that."

"How did your mother take it, you hanging out with elves?"

"She was completely on board. She loves the elves. They are one of our closest allies now."

"She is completely fine with you traveling with three of them?"

"She died a few months ago. She and my father were on their way to pick up a wedding gift for me and their caravan was ambushed. My father was killed first. Captain Oakford, Joshua, my Captain of the Royal Guard, brought her back, but it was too late. Ellavorn couldn't save her. The injuries were too severe and it took too long to get her back to the castle."

Cecilia gave her another funny look. "Why was Ellavorn at your castle?"

"Oh, we were engaged. He was staying there until the wedding. I broke off the engagement after my parents' funeral."

Cecilia stopped dead in her tracks and looked incredulously at Arianna. "You mean to tell me that the *prince* of the elves was going to marry a human?"

"Yes."

Cecilia gave her a look of complete disbelief and began walking again. "Are you a witch? What kind of spell did you cast on him?"

Arianna laughed. "I didn't cast any spell. He saved my life when I was a child. It was kind of love at first sight for both of us. He tried to stay away, but I wouldn't allow that to happen. It just kind of happened, I guess. But, I broke the engagement off when he couldn't save my mother. He ran off and joined an army of pirates. It turns out he joined them to save me from an attack on the kingdom."

"Wow that is some story."

"Well, it's only a part of the story."

"I'm assuming that the other part includes great-grandfather?"

"Well, yes, sort of. While Ellavorn was gone, a Dark Figure has started to threaten my kingdom and myself."

"Wow! That really is some story."

Arianna thought about it for a moment and realized how bizarre the story sounded when she thought about it from an outside perspective and she smiled.

"I know it sounds far-fetched, but it is true. All of it."

"So, what does all of this have to do with great-grandfather?"

"We have to find the descendants of the wizard and bring them back to aid us in the war against the Dark Figure. Armen, Ellavorn's father, instructed us that this would be our only hope."

Cecilia nodded. "Well, I've heard so many stories about Eumetadotos in my life; I would be lying if I said I wasn't curious to see it. I'm not as skilled with spells as my brother, though. My specialty is more on the alchemy side, but I can hold my own."

"You have a brother?"

Cecilia sighed and rolled her eyes. "Yes, a twin brother."

"You don't seem so happy about that."

"We're quite different."

"How so?"

"Sumner is not as forgiving when it comes to our heritage."

Cecilia caught the look of worry on Arianna's face.

"Oh, don't worry; he's not going to hurt you. He isn't stupid enough to do that."

"Are you sure?"

Cecilia nodded. "Yeah, he can be pretty stupid, but that would be a new low for him," she remarked in true sisterly fashion.

"Here we are. This is home."

They stood in front of a large cottage. It was white with a thatched roof and a beautiful garden in the front, which was surrounded by a white picket fence.

Roumpini bounded round the group, stepped over the gate, crushing some flowers as he stepped down, and bounded to the back of the house.

"Roumpini! Be careful! Keandra is going to be furious with you! We also have to get that arrow out of your wing!"

Arianna looked confused. "Why wouldn't you take the arrow out in the woods?"

Cecilia smiled. "Dragon's blood has medicinal properties. It can heal just about any wound. Just a drop and you're right as rain. I didn't want to take the arrow out and waste any of it. It isn't often that they get hurt, and we won't draw blood just to harvest it."

Arianna looked surprised. "I never knew that they had such magical properties."

"Well, I'm not surprised. Not much is known about the dragons from the other realm except that they were dangerous and a nuisance."

"Are these dragons from this realm?"

Cecilia looked uneasy at that question. Luckily, she was

saved by the door banging open behind her.

"There you are! Oh, you brought guests. Come in, come in. My name is Cassidy. I am Cecilia's father."

Cassidy stood in the doorway, surveying his guests. He was tall and had dark brown hair and deep brown eyes that seemed to be taking everything in. He had a playful smile on his lips that hinted at a mischievous nature. Arianna took a liking to him immediately. In a way, he reminded her of Charlie. The thought made her miss her young friend terribly at that moment and she hoped that her journey here was just about over.

Cassidy's eye widened as he took in the sight of the four travelers.

"It cannot be! Are you...are you from Eumetadotos?"

"Father, this is Queen Arianna of Eumetadotos."

"You've brought elves with you!"

"Yes, sir."

"Well, I can't believe my eyes. Come in, come in. Tell me of your journey."

The group made their way into the house.

"Father, I have to tend to Roumpini. He and our new friends had a misunderstanding and he now has an arrow in his wing. I need a jar for his blood."

"A misunderstanding that ends with an arrow in the wing? That sounds like an interesting story. You know where the jars are, Cecilia. Go tend to his wing. Make sure he isn't rolling in the flowers again. Keandra will skin him alive if he crushes any more of them,"

"Yes, Father. Although, we both know that he probably is," she said with a smirk.

"My dragon likes to cause some trouble. I'm sorry if he caused any for you. He really is harmless…unless you're a daisy."

Ellavorn gave him a wary look, and Arianna piped up. "It was actually our fault. We didn't know that he was a *tame* dragon, and he sensed that we meant to hurt him. We're very sorry."

Cassidy waved his hand in dismissal. "No worries. We could use the dragon's blood anyway. We've been running low lately for some reason. I don't know where it has all gone. Now, tell me of why you are here."

The four of them sat down with Cassidy and began to tell him the story of their journey and why they were there to seek help.

"So, you need help to defeat a Dark Figure, do you? Can't do it on your own, can you?"

"We're not certain. We do know that wizarding magic is quite different than elven powers. It wouldn't hurt to have a combination of the two. We also need someone to help young Charlie in his studies as well. He really is quite good," Arianna replied.

Cassidy raised his eyebrows, "You have a wizarding prodigy there, do you?"

"We think so. He was the only one of us that could read the textbooks in the Odigós Domátio."

Cassidy looked stunned. "The Odigós Domátio? You found it?"

"Yes. We found the key and the stone. Charlie was able to decipher everything. The only thing we can't figure out is how to get into the ingredients. There is a barrier or something up to prevent anyone from getting through."

Cassidy started laughing hysterically. "Yes, yes! Grandfather would have done that. He was a smart man, he was."

The four friends exchanged confused looks. Cassidy seemed like he was harmless enough, but he also seemed a little crazy. He was beginning to make all of them slightly uncomfortable.

They heard a roar of pain from the yard.

"No worries. It sounds like Cecilia pulled that arrow from Roumpini's wing."

A look of sympathy crossed Arianna's face.

"Don't worry about it. His wounds will heal up quickly. The dragon's blood heals all wounds."

"Right. Cecilia told us." She gave a weak smile.

Another commotion started in the yard. A woman's voice could be heard yelling.

"Sounds like Keandra is here and Roumpini is in trouble. She is our gardener and she helps with the dragons. She is also a witch. He likes to roll around in her flowers. She gets so mad because she works so hard trying to keep them healthy. I don't understand why she gets so mad. She just has to wave her arms and say a spell to make them right again," Cassidy tried to stifle a smile, but there was also something behind his eyes that the group couldn't quite put their finger on. It was almost like he was jealous of something, or someone.

Cassidy was so busy talking that he didn't hear the back door open and Keandra come in.

"The reason I get so mad, sir, is because magic is not a toy to be played with. It should be used sparingly, as you have been told many times before. You should know all about the consequences." Keandra surveyed the four guests in the kitchen with her emerald green eyes. She was tall, but not as tall as Cassidy, and had hair the color of honey. She turned to address her guests.

"I take it you are the ones that Cecilia was bubbling on about?"

Arianna stood. "Yes, ma'am. I am –"

"I know who you are. I know who all of you are. Cecilia told me of your journey. I do not think that we can help you."

Arianna looked defeated, as did the others.

"Keandra, why would you say such things?"

"Cassidy, they are talking about going to their realm and helping in a war! Lives could be lost. The children could be injured, or die themselves! Why would you risk that? Haven't they lost enough?"

"For a chance to go home!"

"That isn't your home. Your family was exiled here. You were born here. The children were born here. That isn't your home! This place is!"

"It is my grandfather's home."

"Then your father can make the decision as to whether or

not he helps, but I will not take part."

Cassidy had a look of determination on his face, "I guess we'll have to make the journey to ask him, then won't we?"

Keandra rolled her eyes. "If you want to go on that journey, be my guest. Take the flower stomper with you. I will stay here to take care of the others dragons."

Cassidy smiled and danced around, clapping his hands like an excited child. "So, we start another journey. My father lives in the mountains. It is a two day journey by dragon. We'll leave tomorrow morning."

Cecilia came in at the end of his speech. "I want to go too!"

Cassidy smiled at his daughter. "Of course! The more, the merrier."

Cecilia's smile melted into an uneasy glance and she stared through the front doorway as her brother came into the house. She knew that he hated the realm of their ancestors, but she didn't know how he would take to four strangers from that realm being in his family's house at their kitchen table. She also was afraid to guess what his reaction would be when he found out that they would be helping them in their quest. She wasn't so keen on helping elves, but Arianna seemed kind and genuine and she knew that she needed their help.

Sumner skipped up the front steps and into the house and looked around. His face twisted into a look of pure disgust when he saw the guests at the table. The loathing was palpable in his ice blue eyes, the same eyes that his sister has, and hatred seemed to roll from his thin frame in waves. His hands bunched into fists and he growled,

"Eumetadotos," before turning, storming out of the house and slamming the door behind him, leaving everyone in his wake in shock.

Chapter 8

The group looked around at each other, wondering what to do. Cecilia sighed and went after her twin brother, leaving the door open behind her.

"Sumner, wait!"

Sumner whirled around on his sister, fuming mad, hands clenched into fists, and his face red with fury.

"Who brought them here?" He growled out.

Cecilia looked down at her feet and kicked a pebble. "I did."

Sumner's fury rose even more than either of them thought possible.

"How could you do that? You know what they did to our family!"

Cecilia shook her head. "Is living here really so bad? Sumner, we have a good life here. They need our help. They came here seeking grandfather. They want us to go back with them."

Sumner's fury turned to disgust.

"Why would we possibly go back and help them?"

"Because it is the right thing to do. We can go back to Eumetadotos. We can see the places from the stories that we were told all of our lives."

"We would be returning to a place that fears our kind, Cecilia. They tried to kill our ancestors. What makes you think that they won't try to kill us when they're done with us?"

"I don't think that they will, Sumner. Arianna seems nice. I don't fully trust the elves. That female one tried to kill Roumpini."

Sumner's face told Cecilia that she had made a mistake in telling him that part of the story, so she quickly tried to backtrack.

"It was a misunderstanding. They thought he was going to attack, and he thought the same of them. They have never seen one of our dragons, if any at all. The elves have only seen the dragons from Eumetadotos, and they really weren't a great example, to be honest."

"And when they find out about the power of the scales?"

"They won't."

"What makes you so sure that they don't know?"

"They don't. We haven't told them. We won't. That is a family secret."

"Yeah, well, this realm was a family secret too, now wasn't

it?"

"Sumner, I don't know how they found us, but they did. They need help. Great-grandfather left explicit instructions for us to help when they come looking for it."

Sumner curled his lip in disgust and snarled, "Yeah, well, great-grandfather isn't here, now is he?"

Sumner looked back at the house, his mouth drawn tight with rage.

"He wouldn't be here anyway. It's been a hundred years, Sumner. We never met him. Why are you holding onto that anger for so long? He didn't even feel that anger towards them. None of us have, except you."

"Cecilia, do you realize what we could be if we had never left that realm? We could be powerful wizards. We could be doing more than just raising dragons as pets."

"With magic comes power. Power can corrupt, Sumner. You know this. You're starting to sound like him."

Sumner shook his head. "Don't ever compare me to him. I want the power to…never mind. It isn't important."

"Sumner, talk to me. What is it that you want?"

"It isn't important, Cecilia. I'm not going back there. That is final."

Sumner stormed back into the house, leaving his sister behind, speechless. He stormed past everyone in the house and into his room, slamming the door behind him.

Cecilia stared at the house, blinking back tears. She wasn't used to his anger being directed at her. Roumpini peeked his head around the corner of the house, watching his owner. He sensed that she was upset and crept around, resting his enormous head at her feet. She looked down and smiled a sad smile.

"It's ok, boy. I just don't understand his anger is all. I don't know how someone could be so angry at people that he has never met. We have a good life here. I don't know what more he wants."

Roumpini blinked up at her and snorted in agreement. Cecilia smiled and knelt down, leaning into him for comfort.

"I'm glad that we have you. You're a good boy. I should probably go back inside." She patted his face, kissed him on what would be his cheek and stood and started to go back inside. She turned to look at her pet again and smiled a small smile and said, "And stay out of Keandra's flowers. She may have that elf shoot you again!"

She turned and went back to the house as Roumpini snorted his displeasure at being told he wasn't allowed to do his most favorite activity.

As Cecilia stepped back into the house, she could feel the tension in the room. Everyone looked around awkwardly.

"I am sorry about my brother. He harbors a lot of anger towards your kingdom. I wish that he would realize that the past is in the past and that you can only learn from it now. If you hold onto it, it will only turn you bitter. I guess we have different interpretations of the stories from childhood," she said sadly.

Arianna nodded and smiled sympathetically. "It isn't your fault. My ancestors weren't exactly the kindest to your family. I don't know that I would give a warm reception either."

Cassidy sighed. "My son harbors grudges for the slightest things. His anger is what will eventually be his downfall. He must get it under control."

Tanelia was started to get antsy listening to the conversation. She was looking from one face to another. She finally stood up from the table.

"Excuse me. I need some air."

Cecilia made a face at the elf as she passed. The elf could feel the tension rolling off the girl in waves. Arianna noticed the nonverbal exchange and excused herself to follow Tanelia outside.

"Tanelia, wait."

The elf stopped and turned on Arianna with a look in her

eyes that Arianna had never seen before on the elf's face. Her demeanor had changed and she looked at Arianna differently than she ever had before. She seemed almost defeated. The two began to walk around the yard.

"I have never been the subject of that much hatred before."

Arianna looked at her, willing her to go on.

Tanelia sighed. "Is that what it feels like to be on the receiving end of my tirades?"

Arianna gave a half smile and nodded.

"I am sorry, Arianna. I have never thought much about how my hatred would affect anyone else, nor did I care…until now. I have never seen that much disgust directed my way and I realize now that this is how I was treating you. I know that this is hard to believe, but I have begun to care for you and think of you as a…friend."

Arianna smiled, trying not to let the smile get too big. Tanelia noticed and steeled herself again.

"Don't get too excited over that."

Arianna lost her self-control and began to laugh.

"Tanelia, I will take any step forward with you. I care for you as well. I know that there is still some tension towards me, but I hope that we will be able to continue the path that we are on and work towards a stronger friendship. I do care for you a great deal and I trust you with my life."

Tanelia smiled as much of a smile as she would allow without betraying her tough façade.

"Don't worry, I won't tell the others and ruin your image," Arianna said, as though she was reading her mind.

Tanelia shot her a look of disbelief before laughing a short laugh, which shocked Arianna, who had yet to hear the elf laugh.

"Yes, I know how to laugh. I just haven't been given many opportunities to show that lately."

Arianna nodded, understanding. It had been a trying few months for them all. They wandered around some more, lost in their own thoughts. The women turned the corner of the cabin and stopped dead in their tracks, frozen in disbelief at what lay before them.

Chapter 9

The scene in front of Arianna and Tanelia was one that neither would have believed if they hadn't seen it with their own eyes.

Tanelia's hands reached behind her for her bow, but Arianna laid her hand on the elf's arm.

"Stop. That's Roumpini. It looks like he has some friends."

Tanelia sneered in disbelief. "It looks like they've been breeding dragons!"

The two women looked closer at the scene before them. There were at least eight separate dragons, all with different jewel tone scales that sparkled in the sunlight. Some were lying in the sun, soaking up the warmth. Roumpini and a sapphire blue dragon were circling each other. Roumpini would let out a snort, small flames escaping his mouth. The sapphire one would return the snort, however, instead of flames, there were water droplets emitted from its mouth.

Arianna and Tanelia watched in mixed horror and awe as the two dragons would circle each other and then bump each other, seemingly playfully. Two hands clamped down on their shoulders and made them both jump. Arianna let loose a startled scream, which was met with kind laughter.

"I see you have found our dragons," Cassidy said.

Tanelia gave him a look of utter disbelief. "You are breeding dragons?"

"Yes. What you see Roumpini and Lychnítis doing is the mating ritual. They walk in circles with each other, testing each other's strength by the bumping. If they deem each other worthy, they will mate for life. These dragons are quite loyal to each other...and to us as well."

"How did you get their scales to be so beautiful? The dragons in Eumetadotos are quite ugly. These dragons are amazing."

"We are not sure how their scales got to be so vibrant. It may have something to do with the crossing of the realms. We are unsure. My father has books on dragons. You are correct, the dragons of olden days were quite...homely."

Tanelia gave Cassidy a distrustful look. "Dragons have been gone from our realm for a lot longer than these have been around. How did you create them?"

Cassidy smirked. "That is what we all led you to believe. My great-grandfather saved four dragon eggs. He knew that his time in Eumetadotos was drawing to an end. He was fascinated by dragons and believed, as you can see, correctly so, that dragons could be tamed and taught to work peacefully with us. He brought those eggs with him when he crossed realms. These are the fourth generation of dragons. Unfortunately, they do not live as long as they do in their natural realm."

"The dark red one, Lychnítis, you called her, she and Roumpini were breathing fire. But, I saw another breathing water. How do you tell which powers they have?"

"It is all in their scales. The darker blues are water dragons. The red are fire. Those, there," he pointed to the two light blue dragons that were resting peacefully in the sunlight, "Those are ice dragons."

"What about that one?" Arianna pointed to the violet one with scales that matched her own eyes.

Cassidy smiled. "She is beautiful, isn't she? That one is special. She has the capability to emit both fire and ice. We don't know how she does it. She is my personal favorite. We have not been able to replicate her powers in any of our breeding efforts. She is the only one of her kind."

Arianna stood in awe of the dragon, unsure of what to think of the scene that lay in front of her. They were stunningly gorgeous creatures, but still dangerous. Even sweet Roumpini would do some serious damage if he felt that he needed to. It was always believed, by most, that dragons could not be tamed. They are quite enormous creatures. They would be able to wipe out a single village with one step. It seems unnatural that, not just one, but multiple would be lounging and playing like tame house pets.

Cassidy seemed to be reading her mind. "I assure you that they are quite tame. They would not harm anyone without being provoked. We have raised them since the time they were hatched. It is quite a sight to see a dragon hatch and grow."

Arianna was still a bit skeptical. "Why are you breeding dragons?"

Cassidy briefly twisted his face, but only for a second. "Because they have many properties that are beneficial to our lives. You already know of the dragon blood and the qualities that it possesses. There are other benefits as well."

Tanelia, ever suspicious, chimed in, "Like what?"

"There are many benefits. I do not feel that you need to know the majority of them. They are family secrets. The dragon's blood, you only know about because of the circumstances in which you gained that knowledge."

Tanelia's steely gaze fixed on him again. Arianna knew that Tanelia didn't trust Cassidy in the least. She was beginning to distrust him herself. He seemed to be inconsistent in his emotions. One moment, he was warm and welcoming. The next, he was secretive. None of them seemed to trust the elves much.

Cassidy held his head up proudly, watching the dragons with a look on his face that echoed more of a fatherly pride than an owner. Arianna and Tanelia were both starting to feel uncomfortable.

"Would you like to see the rest of them up close?" Cassidy broke the silence while keeping his eyes on the dragons.

Arianna was curious, but also hesitant. Tanelia's face, however, paled. She shook her head. Arianna gave the dragons another curious glance and nodded. Cassidy smiled a smile that could be mistaken as a sneer, which made Arianna a little uneasy. She turned to Tanelia.

"Please don't leave. Please keep watch," she whispered to her.

Tanelia gave her a knowing look and nodded. She had made a decision to stay and keep watch for Arianna before the request was made.

Arianna and Cassidy began to walk down to the dragons. When they got close, a few of them started to become restless at the sight of the newcomer. Cassidy held up his hand and they all settled back into their lounging positions. All except for one. The violet dragon became jitterier as the two walked over to the group, rocking from side to side faster and faster as they moved closer. Arianna began to feel a bit nervous. Cassidy seemed amused by the encounter. Arianna glanced back to see Tanelia watching vigilantly. She felt a little more calm, but not much. The dragon stood suddenly, her gaze focused on Arianna, intently. Arianna froze, intimidated by the powerful dragon, unsure of what might happen.

The dragon studied her carefully for another moment. Arianna could not move, her eyes locked into the dragon's eyes. She had never felt fear so powerful and every muscle in her body froze. The dragon reared up on her hind legs, Arianna's eyes grew wider in fear. The dragon then brought her front feet back down to the ground with a crash, and positioning herself into a lounging position, her head at Arianna's feet, docile. Arianna stood stone still, looking at the dragon, unsure of what to do. She slowly looked at Cassidy, who stood, staring at her, with a look that had a mixture of awe and anger. Her breathing began to even out, once she realized that the threat of danger had passed, at least from the dragon.

"What just happened?"

Cassidy's jaw clenched. She could feel the anger rolling off of him in waves.

"Your Highness, you just acquired yourself a dragon."

Chapter 10

Arianna looked at Cassidy in disbelief as Tanelia came racing up to her, sword drawn, setting the other dragons on edge.

"What do you mean I just acquired a dragon?"

Cassidy looked around at the other dragons, who still seemed agitated by Tanelia's swift entrance. He glared at the sword in her hand, which she promptly sheathed. His anger grew more palpable with every second.

"I mean, what she did just now, that is a dragon's way of pledging their allegiance to you. In essence, she has made you her master. You control her. She will not answer to anyone else."

Tanelia looked from Cassidy to Arianna and back, confusion etched across her face. "So, you mean, she now controls a dragon?"

Cassidy sneered. "Not just any dragon, but the most powerful dragon that we have ever bred."

"But, why me? I don't understand why she would choose me," Arianna whispered, completely confused by the entirety of the events that had just taken place. She was still afraid to move and disrupt the dragon, who had not moved from her position of submission.

Cassidy sighed. "I don't know. I have tried to win her

favor for years with no success."

"How often has this happened," Arianna wanted to know.

"Once. My father has his dragon with him in the mountains. It is the only other time we have seen this happen. They do not pledge themselves to humans very often. It is quite rare."

"What do I do now?"

"You might want to pet her head. She won't move from your feet until you do."

Arianna hesitantly bent down and put her hand out to touch the dragon's head gently. When her fingers made contact with the dragon's scales, in her mind, she saw a burst of pure, white light, much like the magic that would flow from her fingers. She heard a soft, gentle, melodic voice in her mind.

"Thank you, child."

Arianna startled and looked around. The voice began to laugh quietly. The sound was like tiny wind chimes blowing in a soft breeze.

"They cannot hear me. You are the only one who can. I can hear your thoughts as well. I assure you that I mean you no harm."

Arianna looked into the dragon's eyes, realizing in that

moment that they were the same color as her own, letting her many questions flow through her mind.

The laughing continued. "So many questions for one so young. I will answer the burning question at hand. Why did I pick you? A dragon's intuition will tell them if a person is worthy of our allegiance. Only the purest of heart will be chosen. I see in you a heart as pure as pure can be. You are kind, generous, loyal and brave. You are a born leader who has been tasked with a destiny that seems, to you, to be impossible, yet, you persevere relentlessly. I admire that. I cannot tell the future, child, but I can tell you that you are destined for great things. I would care to follow you in your journey."

Arianna's mind grew still as she let the dragon's words sink in. She never broke eye contact with the dragon.

"What is your name?"

"Améthystos."

"Améthystos, I am Arianna. I would be honored if you would join me on my journey."

"Thank you, Arianna. I have pledged my undying loyalty to you. This bond cannot be broken. I know that you are from another realm. It will be imperative that I follow you back. If I do not, my life will end."

Arianna's eyes grew wide in shock and fear.

"Why would you pledge your life to me if you knew that it may cost you your life?"

"Despite what you may have been told about dragons, we look for the good in the world. We wish to align ourselves with the light side. Of course, there are dark dragons who wish to become all-powerful. These are more likely the dragons that you have heard stories about. We are quite peaceful and quite powerful. I believe that anyone would be fortunate to have a dragon on their side."

Arianna smiled a slight smile.

"That is true. I believe I should take all of the help that I can get. My only concern is how to get you into my realm and when we do, will you be lonely?"

"Lonesomeness will not be a concern, I assure you. As for how to get me across that border, do not worry about a solution."

"I fear that Cassidy is not happy with your pledging your allegiance to me."

"Beware of Cassidy's ambition. He is quite charming, however, he does not make the best ally in every situation."

"How do you mean?"

Améthystos paused for a moment, seemingly to gather her

thoughts.

"These people are equivalent to my parents. They have been there for me since I was hatched. I do not wish to speak ill of them, however, humans allow certain factors to corrupt their souls. Cassidy is no different. He can become blinded by his ambition and his quest for power has been becoming more apparent as of late. I fear for his soul."

Arianna was surprised at the last statement.

"But, why?"

"His ambitions are blinding him in many aspects. He looks to control those around him. He seeks more and more power. He has been bound as a wizard."

"What do you mean by bound?"

"He can no longer practice magic, at least in this realm. I do not know if the binding would hold if he crossed realms."

"How did he become bound?"

"His father sensed that the magic was corrupting his mind, as magic can do. It made Cassidy feel invincible, which is not true. His father performed the ritual as to bind his powers so that he could not use them and become even more corrupt. It is why he fled to the mountains, to keep his son safe from the allure of magic. He left Cassidy in charge of the dragons. He did it to protect everyone."

"Who is everyone?"

Améthystos remained silent.

"Améthystos?"

"I cannot divulge that information at this time."

"I will have to respect that."

"Thank you, my queen."

Arianna was surprised.

"How did you know that I am a queen?"

Her question was met by the tinkling bells again.

"There are many things that you will learn about dragons now that we are bonded. But, for now, you must get back to your friends. You must plan your journey to Magus and convince him to come back with you to your realm. I will accompany you on that trip. For now, I will be here awaiting our departure."

The dragon stood up to her full glory, setting off Tanelia's internal alarm. Arianna raised her hand to signal her friend to stop.

"Tanelia, no harm is to come to this dragon."

Tanelia looked startled.

"But, she's a dragon."

"We are bonded. No harm shall come to her as long as I can help it. That is final."

"Oh, great, now you've bonded with a dragon! What else will come of this trip?"

In that instant, the ground beneath Tanelia turned to sheer ice, sending the elf slipping and falling smack on her backside. Arianna heard the slight tinkling of bells in her mind again and did everything she could to hold back the laugh that threatened to escape her mouth. She held out her hand to help Tanelia up off the ground.

"It seems she has a mischievous side, best not to get on her bad side."

"Great, a prankster dragon. Just what we need."

Another sheet of ice formed under Tanelia again, sending her back down on her butt, followed by the tinkling bells. This time, Arianna could not contain the laughter as she helped her friend up off the ground. She turned to address Cassidy, but found that he had already stormed off.

"We should go speak with the others and plan our trip to find Magus."

Arianna looked back at Améthystos again and waved.

"See you soon, child."

Chapter 11

As Arianna and Tanelia approached the house, they found Adasser and Ellavorn outside, waiting for them. They filled them in on what had just happened.

"A *dragon*? You bonded with a *dragon*? Arianna! Dragons are *dangerous*!"

Ellavorn did not take the news of the new acquisition so well. Adasser seemed to contemplate the idea, mulling it over in his mind.

"This is a *terrible* idea, Arianna. Just plain *awful*," Ellavorn kept his tirade going.

"I didn't have a choice, Ellavorn!"

"Actually, I think that this will work to our advantage, Ellavorn," said Adasser finally breaking his silence.

Ellavorn stopped and stared at him in disbelief.

"You can't possibly think that having a dragon accompany us is a good idea? Dragons are dangerous. They're unpredictable."

"They are strong. They are powerful. And, if what this dragon has told Arianna is true, they are loyal and protective. She will be a valuable asset."

A voice came from behind.

"So, it is true. She bonded herself to you?"

Arianna turned to see Cecilia standing there, listening in with an unreadable expression on her face.

"She did."

Cecilia nodded, her expression never changing.

"So, you're going to be taking her with you, then?"

Arianna nodded. "I am."

"Father is very distraught at this development. We didn't realize that you were going to try and steal our dragon when we welcomed you into our home."

Arianna shook her head in disbelief.

"No, Cecilia, I didn't steal her. I didn't ask for this. I didn't even know that a dragon could bond herself to a human. But, now that she has, I will not abandon her."

"Well, that's good, since she'll die if you do."

Cecilia's face softened. "We've raised her since she was a hatchling. I'm going to miss her is all."

Arianna heard the tinkling laughter in her head again, but brushed it off.

"I understand. I am sorry that this will hurt you. I never intended to do anything that would hurt any of you. But, I did not choose this. Améthystos chose to bond herself to me."

"But, why you? She doesn't know you."

The bells chimed in her head again, "Do not tell her our secrets."

Arianna was confused as to why she couldn't trust Cecilia with what Améthystos told her, but decided to trust the dragon.

"I don't know. I wish I had a better answer for you, but I honestly don't."

Cecilia looked as though she didn't believe her for a second, but then her face brightened, "Well, now you really will be the most unstoppable queen ever with your own pet dragon!"

"Cecilia, I am merely looking to protect my people. They are in serious danger right now. I need to find a way to keep them safe. I am not looking to conquer any other kingdoms."

Cecilia smiled brightly. "That is what I was hoping you would say. You are right. A good leader will always protect her people."

"That is exactly right. Right now, the best way for me to do that is to find your grandfather and convince him to return with us."

"Why is it so important to have him return with you?"

"There are some things that we cannot do without his help. The elves' magic is powerful, but it is different from the wizard's magic. I know that my ancestors made some unwise decisions. I just hope that he will not hold those decisions against me now."

Cecilia looked sympathetic. "He won't. He will return to Eumetadotos with you. I know he will."

"How do you know?"

Cecilia laughed. "My grandfather is a very kind person. He's very forgiving. He has talked about going back, but he was always afraid of what would happen if he tried to. I have no doubt that he will go with you."

Arianna felt relieved. "Thank you, Cecilia."

Cecilia smiled.

A thought dawned on Arianna.

"What will your brother say about Améthystos bonding herself to me?"

Cecilia grimaced.

"Father already told us. Sumner is not happy about it. In fact, he is furious."

Arianna and the elves looked uncomfortable.

"I think that we should set up a camp in the woods. We have caused your family enough trouble," Arianna said as the elves nodded in agreement.

"Oh, don't be silly. You can stay in the house."

The group looked at each other uncomfortably.

"Cecilia, we appreciate your offer, but I strongly feel that we should sleep in our camp."

"If that makes you more comfortable," Cecilia grumbled as she turned away.

Arianna caught her arm.

"Cecilia, wait. I am sorry if this hurts your feelings. I am trying to think of how your family feels. Your dragon just bonded herself to a complete stranger. They must feel something about that. I don't want to be the one to rub more salt in the wound."

Cecilia smiled slightly and nodded.

"I understand. Thank you for thinking of their feelings. There is a spot in the woods over there where you can camp. We like to go there a lot when we sleep out."

Cecilia pointed to the entrance to her right.

"I better go in. We will leave at dawn for grandfather's

house. I would suggest not being late. Father hates tardiness," she added the last part as she turned and went back into the house.

The group looked at each other trying to decide if they wanted to sleep where she said. The tinkling bells came through her head again.

"Don't trust any of them, child. Only the old man."

Arianna nodded slightly. "I think we should go over there," she pointed to the left and the group headed that way to set up camp for the night.

Chapter 12

After the group had set up camp, Arianna announced that she was going to visit Améthystos again. Ellavorn expressed his concerns again.

"Arianna, we cannot associate ourselves with dragons."

"Why not?"

"Because they are dangerous! They are unpredictable and greedy and temperamental and they just cannot be trusted."

"Those are the dragons in the stories that you have heard. But, Ellavorn, remember, history is told from the victorious side's view."

"So now we were wrong in eradicating dragons from the realm?"

"I don't know. I wasn't there, and neither were you. I would like to know what happened. These dragons were born here. They know nothing of our realm. The ones that we killed were dangerous."

"Yes, they would burn villages to the ground. They attacked the Glen. They are blood thirsty animals that cannot be trusted."

"I think you're wrong, Ellavorn. Besides, Améthystos

cannot harm me. She is bonded to me. If I die, so does she. Come with me. Meet her. Then form an opinion."

Ellavorn huffed, but then nodded his agreement. They went to tell Tanelia and Adasser where they were going. Tanelia narrowed her eyes and rubbed her backside again, remembering the rump bump that she suffered at the dragon's doing.

"Have fun with that."

Arianna tried not to smile.

"I would like to go and meet the creature," Adasser spoke up.

"Do you really want to meet her?"

Adasser smiled and nodded. "If she is bonded to my granddaughter, of course I do."

Arianna turned to the last holdout. "Tanelia, are you sure you don't want to go?"

Tanelia gave her a look of disbelief. "Absolutely not. I've had enough dragons for one day. It is bad enough we will have to ride on them to get where we need to go."

Arianna stifled a giggle.

"OK, let's go," she turned and led the way to the dragons. When they got there, the dragons were all lazing around, soaking up the rest of the waning sunshine. Arianna scanned the area for Améthystos, spotting her in the corner. Her head rose and she got up to meet the group. Arianna heard Ellavorn and Adasser both suck in a breath.

"She won't hurt you."

The tinkling of bells rang through her head again.

"You brought more elves with you."

"Yes, these are my other companions. I wanted them to meet you to conquer their fears of you."

"I understand. They did not have a good history with my ancestors. Some of my ancestors were not as pure of heart as we are now."

Arianna was amazed that the dragon had knowledge of her own history. "How do you know? You're so young."

The laughter sounded again. "I am young, but dragons are born with their history embedded into our memories already. All of the history of our ancestors are held in our minds."

Arianna looked bewildered.

"Do not fear, child. We know that you were not personally responsible for harming any of us."

"The elf earlier, she helped. That one too," she nodded

towards Adasser.

"He is my grandfather."

"I know, child. I also know that they acted in fear. The dragons that they killed were, in fact, dangerous. They let their greed control them. Your kin did the right thing. Those dragons would have only spiraled out of control. Death was the only option for them in order to protect the well-being of their people...and yours."

A rustling noise sounded from a bush. The group jumped, and the tinkling bells of Améthystos' laughter sounded in Arianna's head again. A baby dragon, no more than three feet tall, popped out, looked at the three strangers, started shifting her feet like she was doing a dance, puffed out a little puff of smoke in Ellavorn's direction, and jumped up and down out of joy and scampered away. Arianna looked at Améthystos in wonder as Ellavorn jumped back.

"She is the youngest. She is still coming into her abilities."

"Does she have a name yet?"

"Not yet. The family comes up with the names. They are waiting to see if she develops abilities similar to mine. She won't. I am the only one of my kind."

"Have there ever been any other dragons with your dual

ability?"

"No. There may never be again. Much like you, I am fulfilling a prophecy. You see, there is more to our bond than just your pure heart, child. We both have a destiny to fulfill and our paths are linked. We depend upon one another to fulfill them."

"You know about my destiny?"

"Child, I know everything about you. Our minds are linked. We can share thoughts, feelings, history, everything. I wanted to explain that to you earlier, but we didn't have the time. Our destinies are intertwined. In order for both of us to fulfill them, we must work together."

"What is your destiny?"

"Freedom for my kin."

"What do you mean?"

"We are dragons. We do not care to be kept as pets. No matter how gentle we may seem, we are still creatures who want to be free. The family keeps us here. We wish to return to your realm as we did in the past."

"All of you?"

"Yes, child. All of us."

"I don't know that the Wizards will allow it. I mean, I am

willing to try, but I do not know how to convince them."

The tinkling bells sounded again.

"You get us to your realm. We will work on the rest."

"OK. We can do that."

"Arianna," Ellavorn called her name.

Arianna turned to face Ellavorn and Adasser.

"It is OK, you can tell them. They are trustworthy. And, besides, you love the prince."

Arianna turned back and shot her a semi-embarrassed look. Améthystos' ability to read her mind was becoming a little disconcerting.

The dragon laughed again.

Arianna turned back to the men and began to explain.

"When Améthystos bonded herself to me, it opened a link between our minds. I can speak to her that way."

Ellavorn looked like he was about to faint.

"So, you can *talk* to dragons too?"

"Just her. I don't have that link with the other dragons."

Adasser was listening, fascinated.

"How can this be? I never knew that a dragon was capable of such things."

Arianna smiled. "I didn't either."

The ground began to rumble slightly as another dragon approached. They looked around and saw a gorgeous, sapphire colored dragon coming towards them.

"That is Zafeíri. He is the most powerful water dragon of all of us."

Arianna relayed the information to the others. They all stood stock still, watching every move that the dragon made. He went up to each one and sniffed them all, nuzzling Arianna's stomach a bit when he did.

"He knows that we are bonded. This is his way of showing his loyalty to you as well."

Arianna reached over to pet his enormous nose. "Why would he show loyalty to me if I am not bonded to him?"

The tinkling bells sounded again. "Because he shows loyalty to those that his queen is loyal to, and he is my mate."

Arianna was shocked. "Wait, you're the queen of the dragons? If he is your mate, that would make him king."

"That is correct. By bonding myself to you, I have made a treaty between us. None of these dragons will harm you so long as they are loyal to me."

"Arianna! What. Is. It. Doing?"

Arianna and Améthystos turned to see Zafeíri start the bonding ritual in front of Ellavorn,

"Ellavorn, stay still!"

When he was finished, Zafeíri bowed before Ellavorn's feet.

"You have to touch him. Ellavorn, it looks like you've acquired a dragon as well."

Ellavorn fainted. Améthystos laughed. Zafeíri looked at his queen, confused.

Arianna and Adasser both rushed over to Ellavorn's side to revive him.

"Oh, good, it was a dream. No pet dragon."

Arianna laughed. "Well, no, you have to touch him, Ellavorn."

"I don't want a dragon! Dragons are dangerous!"

"Ellavorn! Stop behaving like a child. Touch the dragon and form that bond! This is important!"

Arianna was starting to get irritated with him.

Ellavorn stood, closed his eyes and reached out to touch the dragon. When he did, his eyes flew open, and he froze, listening to what the dragon was telling him. He looked at Arianna in disbelief at what he was hearing.

Arianna smiled at him, understanding the feeling that she, herself, had just experienced a few hours ago. It was a lot to take in all at once.

"Arianna, I'm talking to a dragon. A real dragon."

"Ellavorn, you are bonded to this dragon."

Ellavorn looked like he was about to faint again. He sat back down and Zafeíri laid his head down next to him. His eyes soulful, looking at Ellavorn.

Arianna could hear Améthystos' voice again.

"Zafeíri is apologizing to Ellavorn. He knows that Ellavorn's heart is as pure as you and he wanted to never be parted from me. If he bonded himself to the elf, he would never have to be parted from me."

"How do you know that?"

"He is my mate. We can read each other's minds as well as yours."

Arianna changed her attention back to Ellavorn. He was still looking at the dragon, but looking a little less bewildered and a little more curious. Arianna didn't know what they were talking about, but the dragon seemed to be talking the elf round.

Suddenly, the dragon popped up onto all fours and bowed his head. Ellavorn looked at Arianna shyly, and then climbed up onto the dragon's back. Arianna watched in stunned disbelief as Ellavorn settled himself down and the dragon stretched his wings and took off into the sky.

Améthystos began to giggle. "Would you like to go for a ride as well, child?"

Arianna's eyes grew as big as saucers and nodded, looking at Adasser, who seemed completely at a loss as to what was happening.

"Your grandfather may come too."

"Adasser, let's take a ride."

Adasser looked terrified as he looked at the ground and up to the dragon and back.

Arianna grabbed his wrist and dragged him up behind her. They settled in and Améthystos beat her wings and they took off into the sky after Ellavorn and Zafeíri.

Chapter 13

As they rose high up in the sky, Arianna felt Adasser's grip around her waist tighten more and more the higher that they went into the sky. She tried not to laugh at the thought of the fierce elf afraid of flying.

They evened out and Arianna caught sight of Ellavorn and Zafeíri. Améthystos seemed to be trying to catch up to them. When she did, it seemed that the two dragons were delighted to be in one another's company. They circled each other, seemingly to outdo one another, all while keeping careful track of their passengers.

Arianna was delighted with the ride. Adasser seemed to not be as enthralled as she was. She heard him muttering under his breath, but she couldn't make out what he was saying. She tried to catch a glimpse of Ellavorn's face, but couldn't.

The dragons seemed to have their fill of flying and began their descent. They flew down to where the group had set up camp. Tanelia had started setting up camp while the rest were on their flight. The dragons settled on the ground and Arianna, Adasser and Ellavorn climbed down to the ground. Arianna turned to look at Adasser and was met by her grandfather's extremely pale face.

"That was not my idea of a good time. Excuse me for a

moment."

Adasser disappeared into the woods before Arianna could say anything.

She raced over to where Ellavorn stood. He seemed to be locked in conversation with Zafeíri and more comfortable with the idea of a dragon bonding himself to him. Zafeíri seemed to take notice of her before Ellavorn and must have said something to him because Ellavorn turned to her and smiled. She returned the smile and walked over to him.

"That was a wild ride, wasn't it?"

He nodded. "It definitely was. I never in all of my life imagined that I would be riding a dragon."

"Neither did I, yet, here we are."

Tanelia came stomping out of the camp to see what the commotion was about.

"What the—what is going on here? You brought *dragons* back? Where is Adasser? They didn't eat him, did they?"

Arianna and Ellavorn laughed.

"No, Tanelia. Adasser didn't seem to like the ride. He went into the woods for a moment alone."

"So, there's two dragons. Did that one bond himself to you

too?"

"Well, no."

"He bonded himself to me," Ellavorn spoke.

"*What? Ellavorn!* An Elf cannot have a dragon tagging along! Our people would kill him if you took him back to the Glen!"

"I will take care of that. There will be a decree that none of these dragons are to be harmed. Tanelia, they are not like the ones from our stories."

"Ellavorn, I do not like this. They are *dragons!* Our people are trained to *kill* dragons with no questions asked."

"Tanelia, I am aware of all of this. I am also aware of the fact that this dragon chose me. He made a bond to protect me and, therefore, I will return the favor, or I will sacrifice myself trying."

"First a human and now a dragon. I feel like I don't even know you anymore."

"You don't, Tanelia. I have come to realize that things are changing everywhere. Things are not always black and white. Many times, there are a multitude of shades of gray. You cannot live your life in a polarized manner. If you do, you will miss out on many experiences. I cannot force you to change your views, however, I can declare protection orders on Zafeíri, which is this dragon's name, by the way."

Tanelia looked defeated. She looked at the ground and shook her head sadly.

"I am trained to protect the Glen. I am trained to protect you. That is my job. Surely, you can understand that? In addition, our previous relationship taints my views some as well. I still care for you quite deeply, Ellavorn. I know that we will never be together, but I cannot turn those feelings off, no matter how hard I try. I will always love you, Ellavorn, it is why I try to keep you especially safe."

Ellavorn look at her with sympathy.

"I am sorry, Tanelia. I never meant to hurt you—"

"I know you didn't."

"I wasn't finished. I never intended to fall in love with a human. I know the views that our people hold towards them. I held them myself. But, Tanelia, humans are not what we make them out to be," while he said that last part, he glanced over at Arianna who looked to be deep in conversation with Améthystos, and he smiled at her.

"There are kind humans, Tanelia."

"I agree that she is," Tanelia sighed and shrugged her shoulders, "I actually kind of like her. It must be the Elf part of her."

Ellavorn chuckled a bit.

"Tanelia, I cannot change my feelings towards either of you, and I can't say that I would if I could. I love you still, but in a very different way. You are a wonderful protector. I would never change that about you. However, we do have the issue of the dragon."

Tanelia shook her head in disbelief.

"It would have had to have been a dragon."

Ellavorn laughed again.

"Have you ever known me to do anything the easy way?"

Tanelia cracked a small smile and indicated to Arianna.

"Maybe the two of you really do belong together after all," and she began to stomp away, in true Tanelia fashion.

Ellavorn watched her go and laughed.

Chapter 14

After landing, Arianna stood talking to Améthystos about what to expect next.

"How are we going to explain this to the Wizards? They weren't very happy when you bonded yourself to me. Now Zafeíri has bonded himself to Ellavorn."

"And others will bond to the other two."

Arianna froze.

"Excuse me?"

"Child, this is a necessity. If we bond ourselves to you, they have no choice than to let us go with you."

"But, there are only four of us. There are at least a dozen of you."

"Yes, I know. We can get the others to cross as well."

"How? I can't sneak an entire dragon into a completely different realm! They're bound to notice that!"

The tinkling of the bells sounded again.

"Open your mind to mine. You have the answers. You just choose not to look for them."

Arianna looked into Améthystos' eyes, concentrating hard. The world around her faded and she began to watch the history of the dragons unfold before her. She saw that everything that Améthystos had told her was true. The peace and destruction alike, until the peaceful dragons realized that they were outnumbered.

Amidst all of the turmoil, a man in a hooded cloak had appeared to speak with the dragons. The hood fell back and his face was revealed. He stood tall with his hair black as ebony and eyes to match, however, where Iron Demon's eyes are cold, this man's eyes were friendly and welcoming. There was no trace of malice in them at all.

"I am Aldore, Wizard of Eumetadotos. I come in peace."

Arianna gasped. She was looking at the banished wizard directly.

The dragon who seemed to be the queen at the time was a bright green color, unlike any of the dragons she had seen here. She nodded as if to encourage him to continue.

"I know that your species is in danger, as am I and my family. I come seeking an alliance with you. I will be forced to flee this realm in time and I have heard of a power that dragons have in order to aid this."

The queen nodded again for him to continue.

"I will be in need of another realm where my family could live in peace. I would like to strike an alliance between us and bring your kind with me. I know that many of your kind have turned to the darkness, but the ones who are still true, I would like to give them a chance."

The queen stood and walked over to Aldore. Arianna watched in anticipation. The enormous dragon began doing the bonding ritual. And laid her head at Aldore's feet. Aldore placed his hand on her head and a look of surprise spread across his face, then, he smiled and nodded.

The queen stood up and plucked an emerald scale from her flank. She handed it to Aldore and it shimmered and flashed, much like the scale that Arianna had found. Arianna gasped as Aldore stroked the scale in a clockwise manner and the color began to swirl. A flash appeared and a portal opened with a view of the area that the group was currently standing in. It did not contain a house or any of the grounds as it stood now. Aldore looked at the dragon in shock and she nodded.

"It is perfect."

Aldore turned to look at the dragon and she started to speak, her voice, almost just a whisper on the wind.

"When the time comes, you will escape here and continue your bloodline and mine."

Aldore looked surprised, "Will you not join me? I thought that when a dragon bonds itself to a human, they must not be parted."

The dragon seemed sad. "No, I will not join you. My kind will be attacked shortly before you leave. None of us will survive. However, I have hidden away four eggs, one from four different dragons. I need you to promise me that you will take them with you and continue my species in this other realm. Teach them the ways of the light. Do not allow them to turn to the darkness. A dragon's heart is naturally led to the light, but the darkness can easily corrupt us. Do not allow this to happen to my kin."

Aldore nodded and seemed sad that his new friend would not be accompanying him on this journey. "I will do everything I can to prevent the darkness from creeping into their hearts."

The dragon nodded and motioned with her head toward a nest in the corner of the room. Aldore made his way over to the nest and found four eggs, just as the dragon had said.

"Where should I hide them? Surely, they will be found in Eumetadotos and the king will have them destroyed."

"Take them to the other realm now. Hide them well. When it is your time to cross over, find them, hatch the babies and raise them. My kin will be instrumental in helping to save that kingdom in time. She will be very powerful."

Aldore looked unsure. "How will I get back?"

"Use the scale. It will take you between realms whenever you wish."

"Is it true that if a dragon bonds itself to a human that it must stay close to the human or perish?"

"Yes."

"Then, if I take these eggs to that other realm, you will die."

"My time is coming to an end. The kings grow ever more fearful of my brethren, and rightfully so. I am the last of the dragons that have not been corrupted. All of the rest have turned to the darkness. I cannot save them now."

She thought for a moment, "I will accompany you to the other realm so that you can hide the eggs. My fate is drawing near, however, and I do not have much time left. We should leave quickly."

Aldore nodded in agreement and went to gather the eggs. When he had gathered them all together, the dragon lowered herself so that he could climb up and settle himself in.

"What should I do now?"

"Rub the scale."

He did and the portal opened itself again. The dragon walked through the portal and lowered herself again to allow Aldore to climb down. They found a place for all four of the eggs and Aldore pulled out the scale again.

"I will not be going back with you."

Aldore's eyes snapped to the dragon.

"What do you mean?"

"I mean, I will stay here with the eggs."

"But – you will die when I cross realms."

"Yes, I will. However, it is what needs to be done for the sake of both of our bloodlines. I would rather die here of a broken bond than to be slain in a most undignified manner. When I die, the scale will be useless. Find the realm jumping spell and use it to find me and my eggs."

Aldore walked back to the dragon and held his hand up. The dragon lowered her head and nuzzled his hand.

"Thank you for helping me and my family to escape," Aldore said quietly.

"Thank you for continuing my bloodline," the dragon responded, "Now, go, you must get back before it is discovered that you have crossed realms."

Aldore opened the portal again, walked over, turned and gave the dragon one last look.

"Please remember to keep them in the light. Do not let them turn to the darkness. We need them and all of their descendants to stay light."

"You have my word that I will do my best."

"That is all that I can ask of you."

Aldore stepped through the portal, and as it closed, he heard the dragon let out her last deafening roar. He looked down at the scale and it shimmered green and then went dark.

Chapter 15

Arianna's body jerked as the vision ended. She looked up at Améthystos with tears in her eyes.

"Do not weep, child, my grandmother knew what she was doing. She had to stay behind so that the wizard had no ties to her. The other dragons would have sensed it and made him a target. She was the last of the Dragons of the Light. The others had turned to the darkness. Their hearts turned ugly and there was no turning them back.

She also knew that when the humans found her, that they would not understand that she was not dark. They would have killed her anyway. She died with dignity, saving our species."

Arianna nodded and looked at Améthystos in confusion, a thought coming to her,

"Is that why the dragons in our history were ugly? Did their hearts turn the color of their scales?"

Améthystos smiled. "You are quite intuitive. Yes, a dragon's heart is reflected in their scales. If they are light dragons, they will keep their beautiful colors. However, if their hearts turn dark, their scales will turn to match their hearts."

"And the scales, they can open portals to other realms?"

The dragon smiled, "Yes, child, they can, but we found that only while the dragon is living. Once the dragon dies, the power ceases to work."

"That's why the wizard needed the spell in order to leave the realm."

"Yes. He would have had to enact a spell in order to find this realm."

"What became of your great-grandmother after he crossed to this realm?"

"He found her bones and erected a monument to her. Would you like to see it?"

"Yes, please! I would love to see it. Let me tell my friends where we are going."

Arianna went back to her friends and relayed the story that she had just learned to Adasser, Tanelia, and Ellavorn. They all sat in surprised silence at what they had just been told.

Adasser spoke first, "Well, it makes sense now how the dragons can to be in this realm. I never knew that their scales were so powerful."

"Améthystos is going to take me to see the monument that Aldore erected in her grandmother's memory. Would and of you like to come with us?"

Adasser's face went pale. "We won't be flying, will we?"

Arianna laughed, "I'm not sure."

"I don't think I want to take that chance."

Ellavorn stood up. "I will go. I would like to see it."

They looked at Tanelia.

"Don't look at me. I have no interest in dragons."

Arianna shrugged with a giggle and said, "OK. Let's go, Ellavorn."

Ellavorn offered her his elbow and it took her by surprise. She looked at it for a second and linked her arm through his. It felt right and she felt that familiar comforting feeling that she had always felt being with him. She looked up and him and smiled and he returned that smile. They started walking off to where the dragons were waiting.

Upon arrival, Améthystos's voice ran in Arianna's ears, "I knew that you would find your way back to each other."

Arianna smiled, "Well, nothing is official yet. We are just walking together right now."

Améthystos laugh tinkled in her ears.

With that, Zafeíri appeared beside her. Arianna looked sideways at Ellavorn, who had a slight smile on his face. He nodded to Zafeíri and the dragon nodded back to him.

"I'm glad to see that you've opened your mind and accepted your dragon."

Ellavorn chuckled, "Well, I'm still getting used to the idea, but he's growing on me."

Arianna smiled broadly.

The dragons lowered themselves so that their bonded humans could climb on.

Ellavorn asked, a little shakily, "Are we flying this time?"

Zafeíri shook his head.

Améthystos said to Arianna, "Your beloved doesn't seem to like to fly. Don't worry, we will walk this time. It isn't far."

Arianna laughed, "I don't think elves like to fly. Adasser turned a very specific shade of green when we asked him."

Améthystos's laugh tinkled in her ear yet again. "Elves are funny creatures."

Arianna smiled. "They are just used to their own ways. They don't really associate with many other races."

"Yes, the mortality complex. They don't want to risk falling in love with a human and tainting their mortality, am I correct?"

"That is correct."

"And yet, two of the three elves here now have done just that, fallen in love with a human, one openly agreed to marry her. He must love you immensely."

Arianna blushed.

"Well, I know that he did. I'm not so sure now. I messed up pretty badly."

Améthystos nodded.

"He understands. He is still hurt, but he understands. He still loves you."

"Did Zafeíri tell you that? I didn't know that dragons were fans of gossip."

Améthystos laughed again.

"No, we don't care much for gossip. I can tell by the way that he looks at you. Child, he loves you very, very much. Do not let too much time go by before you tell him how you feel about him. He is a big part of helping you fulfill your destiny. Not just his healing power, but his love for you."

"How did you know he is a healer?"

"Most dragons do not care much for gossip, however, we do share pertinent information, such as our bonded human's powers, young Warrior Queen.”

Arianna giggled a bit.

“I wish I had known sooner. I wish that my mother had known.”

“Sometimes, things are better left unknown for the time being, child. Things come to light when they need to. Your mother never really needed to know.”

“It would have been helpful that day in the woods.”

Améthystos stayed quiet for a moment.

“Yes, that would have been beneficial for your parents and their guards. However, and I know that you don’t want to hear this, we all have our moment when our time with the living is complete. Your parents’ time was together. Could you have imagined them being without the other?”

Arianna thought for a second and shook her head, “No. My parents were so in love and never wanted to be parted from each other. Ever.”

Améthystos smiled, “They went together, as they were meant to. In addition, their deaths spurred you on to become the woman that you are becoming. You have found an immense well of strength within yourself, and you discovered your powers and your true heritage. Do you believe that you would have been able to do any of that while they were still alive?"

"Well, no, I don't. I still wish that they were here to help me."

"We will always miss the ones who have moved on to the other side, especially those that are so dear to us. We will never forget them, but we must learn to accept that they are no longer physically here for us to guide us every day. We can only dig into our hearts and feel their guidance.

Arianna understood what Améthystos was telling her, however, it didn't help to lessen the pain in her heart any.

"We are here, child."

Arianna looked up to see a beautiful white stone memorial with a dragon's image engraved on the front. She glanced over at Ellavorn and they both dismounted their dragons at the same time and walked over to the stone.

They walked over to the stone together in silence. Arianna reached her hand out to touch the cold white stone and she saw a flash of bright white light and froze. She felt as though she was falling through space as the scene in front of her eyes changed. The stone was gone and a large hole was opened in front of where the stone had stood. It was daylight.

She heard a noise and looked to her right, where she saw

Aldore pulling a cart with the dragon's body to the hole. She realized that she was attending the dragon's funeral. Aldore approached the hole, seemingly unaware that Arianna was there. He whispered a spell and the dragon's body floated from the cart to the hole, and he began to fill the hole with dirt.

When the hole was full, he waved his hand and the white stone was erected in front of him. Arianna thought that he would have simply walked away, however, he reached into his cloak and pulled something out of his pocket. It flashed red in the sunlight. Her breath caught in her throat. It looked like the key to the Odigós Domátio, except larger, the size of a dagger. She stepped closer to get a better look at it when Aldore plunged it into the earth.

"Protect this dagger, great dragon. There will be a time when we will need it again to defeat the great evil that will threaten our homeland. Only the one from the Elven Prophecy will be able to claim it."

Aldore whispered some words and the dagger glimmered and then disappeared. He turned to where Arianna stood, but it was like he was looking through her.

"The heart of the dragon will bring forth the dagger."

He then turned and walked away. As he did, Arianna opened her eyes to see Ellavorn's worried face looking into her own.

"Wh-what happened?" Arianna asked.

"I don't know. You fainted when you touched the stone."

"I had a dream. The heart of the dragon will bring forth the dagger. Améthystos, does this mean anything to you?"

The dragon shook her head no.

Arianna walked over to the stone again, hesitant to touch it again. She placed her fingertips on the image of the dragon and the outline flashed the same way that the dagger did in her vision. She quickly jerked her hand back.

Ellavorn's eyes grew wide, "Arianna, did you see that?"

"Yes, I did."

She reached out again and brushed her fingertips across the image again, resulting in the same flash. She pulled her hand back again.

"The heart of the dragon…"

She examined the image some more and noticed that one of the scales was shaped like a heart. She put her hand out to touch it, again, hesitantly. When her hand made contact, the image flashed again, but this time, she did not pull her hand away. Instead, she traced the image to the heart shaped scale and there was a flash that blinded her for a second. She heard Ellavorn gasp behind her. She turned around and saw the dagger planted in the ground, right where Aldore had plunged it. She walked over and yanked it out of the ground. It looked exactly like the key back in Eumetadotos.

Ellavorn exclaimed, "I can't believe it! It's the Stiléto me fteró drákou!"

Chapter 16

"Arianna, this is incredible. The Stiléto me fteró drákou has not been seen since the wizard left!"

A look of realization crossed over Ellavorn's face, followed by worry.

"You truly are the one from the prophecy. There is no other explanation for this. We all thought that you were, but this solidifies those suspicions. You are the one who will save us all from this creature that taunts us."

"It seems like that is so, Ellavorn," Arianna replied nervously.

"We must get back and tell Adasser and Tanelia," Ellavorn was growing more excited and anxious by the moment.

"We will, Ellavorn. Just be patient," Arianna said while moving the dagger slowly.

As she moved it, the blade caught the light from the moon and it shimmered. She felt a warm power radiating up her arm. It was warm and wasn't unpleasant.

"Swing the dagger, child," the sound of Améthystos's voice tinkled in her ears.

Arianna looked at the dagger, hesitantly, and then looked into the face of the dragon, who nodded to her.

She held the hilt in her hand and swung the dagger with a flick of her wrist and it began to glow. She began to feel a pulse coming from the handle of the dagger in the middle of the lotus flower. Arianna dropped it at her own feet and the glow extinguished and the pulsing sensation stopped.

"What happened? What was that?"

"The dagger is meant to glow for the true savior. It has many powers, most of which are unknown at this point."

"How does it glow like that?"

"It was forged in dragon fire, child. Our fire has many magical uses. This is a very powerful weapon. It is almost impossible to destroy."

"Almost impossible?"

The dragon's laugh tinkled again. "Yes, almost. It is a rather difficult task, but it can be accomplished. Make no mistake, however, a weapon forged in dragon's fire is formidable."

Arianna picked up the dagger a swung it again, causing it to glow brightly. This time, however, she held on to it, admiring the beauty of it. Just like the key that they found to the Odigós Domátio, the key looked like it was made from one solid ruby. It didn't feel like a ruby, though. It felt different.

"What is this made of, Améthystos?"

The dragon lowered her head to inspect it further.

"This dagger is made from a ruby, however, it is infused with dragon's blood, and then forged in dragon's fire. I may have been mistaken. I don't know if this dagger can be destroyed after all."

"How do you know there is dragon's blood infused in it?"

"Look closely at it, child."

Arianna brought the dagger closer to her face to inspect it closer, but she didn't see anything out of the ordinary, aside from it being forged from a ruby. She shook her head.

"Focus on it closer, child."

Arianna felt frustrated, but she looked again.

"Focus on the blade and look very closely."

Arianna squinted at the blade and started to notice that it looked like small veins running through it. She ran her finger along the flat side of the blade and found that it looked like a circulatory system throughout the entire blade. She gasped and looked at Améthystos, who smiled.

"When dragon fire is forged into a weapon, it takes on a life of its own."

"The handle, it felt like a heartbeat when I held it."

Améthystos nodded again, "Yes that is the heart of the

weapon. It brings life to the rest of it."

"Are there many weapons like this?"

The dragon slowly shook her head. "None that are known. We didn't know that this was made with dragon's blood until this moment."

"How can that be? Don't dragons pass their history down to each newborn dragon? You said you were born with knowledge of all of dragon history."

"I do not know how this is possible. I can only imagine that someone forged this without dragon knowledge. It has been in the wizarding family for centuries. Perhaps the old man will know."

Arianna swung the blade again, feeling the pulse in the handle and causing it to shimmer in the moonlight, although, at this point whether it was the moonlight causing the shimmer or the dragon magic that seemed to inhabit the dagger was anybody's guess. The sheer beauty of it, however, was unmistakable.

Arianna walked back over to the dragon's stone and touched the etching again. The etching stayed the same. The shimmer that was there seemed to have vanished.

"Thank you," Arianna whispered as she stood to leave.

It was then that she noticed a flickering in the forest.

"Fire!" She yelled.

"Améthystos, Zafeíri, Ellavorn, there's a fire in the forest!"

Ellavorn started to run full speed towards the fire with Zafeíri chasing after her. Arianna began to run as well, but Améthystos's voice tinkled in her ears again.

"Child, stop!"

Arianna turned towards her with a bewildered look on her face.

"We have to get help! The fire will destroy the forest. My grandfather and my friend are in there."

"No, child, they are safe. This is no ordinary fire."

Arianna was confused.

"What do you mean this is no ordinary fire?"

"Child, that fire was started by this very dragon. You see, dragon eggs need dragon fire in order to hatch. No other fire burns strong enough in order for that to happen. She started this fire in order for the eggs to hatch when Aldore returned. Dragon fire also does not extinguish on its own. It will burn forever if it is allowed."

"So, this fire has been burning for over a century?"

"One hundred and fifty years."

"But, the wizard has only been gone from Eumetadotos for a

hundred or so years."

"Yes, he did not leave right away after being told about this realm. Remember, when she died, her scale died with her. Aldore had to find the spell in order to cross over to another realm. It took him a long time to find that. She knew that once she died, that there would be no way to hatch those eggs without dragon fire. She started this fire with the foresight that he would come back and use it for its intended purposes. Aldore kept this fire alive and commanded that all dragon eggs henceforth in this realm shall be hatched from this very fire."

"So, that is where you were born?"

Améthystos smiled.

"It is where all of us were born, child."

"I would like to see it."

"As would I, child."

Arianna and Améthystos walked over to the fire, which was encircled by bricks that looked like they used to be white, but were now charred around the edges due to being in close proximity of such intense heat for so long.

The fire was, indeed, hotter than any Arianna had ever felt and she noticed that there were two eggs in the center of the fire. The eggs looked as though they were burning red from the intense heat.

"Améthystos, are those dragon eggs?"

Améthystos sighed.

"They are my children. Mine and Zafeíri's."

Arianna's eyes brimmed with tears.

"You're going to be a mother?"

Améthystos nodded.

"I am, child. I am. I don't know that I will ever be able to meet my children, though."

Realization hit Arianna like a ton of bricks.

"Why would you pledge yourself to me and leave them behind? Why would you do that, knowing that you may not make it back? You could leave them motherless!"

Améthystos sighed. Arianna looked up and saw tears in her eyes. Those tears spilled down her face.

"I had to. It is our destiny to fight this together. You are human still. You have elven abilities, but you are still mostly human. You need my help and the help of the dragons as well. You cannot fight this alone. I had to pledge myself to you in order to help you. I knew that this day would come and I know the risks that I am taking. What good is it to save myself for my children if, by doing that, I destroy the very world that we, together, are destined to protect?"

"But, your children…"

"They will be born knowing that their mother did what she had to do. They will be proud of my choices, just like I am proud of hers. We dragons do not see things from an emotional stand point. We see things as right or wrong. We take pride in doing the right thing."

"Unless they turn?"

"Unless they turn. Then the only pride that they have is what is best for them."

Arianna reached up and stroked Améthystos's scales.

"Have any dragons turned in this realm?"

"Only one. He died. It broke my heart to see it happen."

"I'm so sorry. What happened?"

"He pledged himself to Cassidy before Cassidy was bound. He teetered on the edge of madness and Magus saw it happening. He bound Cassidy before he slipped too far onto that side. When Cassidy was bound, the magic that the dragon had tethered to was locked away. In essence, the magic is what we bind ourselves to. With that being gone or locked away, it is the same as the human dying. A piece of them is dead. When that happened, the dragon was not able to feel that connection anymore. He died the instant that Cassidy was bound."

Arianna listened closely and could hear the pain in Améthystos's voice as she told the story.

"Wait, Cassidy didn't tell me about this. He said that the only dragon that had bound itself to someone was Magus's dragon."

"Cassidy will lie to you in order to hide family secrets. He will hide what he feels he must. I do not know how he feels in regards to this dragon, whether he feels regret or if he simply just doesn't care. He was bound to him and he was reckless with his magic. It corrupted him, and in turn, the dragon became corrupted and needed to be executed. We, collectively, decided not to pledge ourselves to anyone again unless it was to fulfill a destiny."

"It must have been so hard to see that. I'm sorry that you did."

"Thank you, child. I will never forgive Cassidy for what he did to my father."

Arianna's breath caught.

"Your father was the dragon who turned?"

"Yes, child. This is why we do not bind ourselves to humans now. We know how easily they can be corrupted and we do not wish to turn that same way. We do not wish to suffer that same fate. You see, when a dragon binds themselves to you, we are able to pull from each other's powers. Being bound to me will only increase your own power, as it will mine. If the person turns to the darkness, the dragon will soon follow. This is what happened to my father."

"What was his name?"

"We do not speak his name anymore. Once a dragon turns, he has turned his back on his family, and in essence, we turn our backs on him. His name is never to be spoken by us again."

"And the human? Is it possible to save them?"

"Cassidy has come back from the brink of insanity, however, he is still obsessed with having power again. I cannot say what would happen if that were ever to occur."

"What about me? I am mostly human."

"You are also part elf and you are the chosen one. That makes you unique. In addition, you hold the Stiléto me fteró drákou in your hand. That proves that you are the chosen one. Any dragon would be honored to pledge themselves to you."

Arianna blushed as she looked at the dagger in her hand. She had forgotten that she was holding it.

Améthystos said, "We should get back to the site and get some sleep. We have to leave early in the morning and Cassidy does not like tardiness."

Chapter 17

The next morning, Arianna and Ellavorn stumbled out of their perspective tents looking like zombies. Adasser and Tanelia gave them both interested glances.

"Rough night?" Tanelia asked.

Arianna sighed, "You could say that."

She reached into the tent and pulled out the Stiléto me fteró drákou. Adasser and Tanelia both froze in their tracks, shocked at the sight of the legendary dagger.

Adasser was the first to find his voice. "Wh-where did you find that? It had been rumored to have been lost forever."

"Améthystos and Zafeíri took Ellavorn and me to the original dragon's grave site. I touched the etching and it appeared for me."

Adasser looked the dagger over again. "It is as beautiful as I remember it."

"Adasser, do you feel the heartbeat of the dagger too?"

Adasser looked at her, confused.

"What do you mean, the heartbeat?"

"When I hold the hilt, I feel the pulsing. Améthystos said that the ruby is infused with dragon's blood and that it has its own heartbeat."

"Arianna, you feel the heartbeat because you are the rightful owner now. Aldore passed this down to you. It does not surprise me that you can feel a heartbeat within the hilt."

"Améthystos says that this proves that I am, indeed the one from the prophecy."

"Améthystos is correct. Arianna, I think it would be best if we kept this information to ourselves for now. I just have a feeling that we should not tell the wizards."

"You don't trust them?"

"Not at this point in time, no, not entirely."

Arianna nodded in agreement.

"Cassidy is bound."

Adasser's jaw dropped.

"They bound a wizard?"

"Améthystos told me. Apparently, the magic drove him almost insane. He couldn't handle it. Magus bound him. Améthystos said that he seems to have gotten better, but she is unsure of what would happen if he got his powers back."

"It is probably best if we don't find out, and we should do what we can to stay on his good side. A bound wizard can be very volatile."

"He is already angry that two of the dragons have pledged themselves to Ellavorn and myself. I will try not to give him any more reasons to dislike me."

"Somehow, it is not Cassidy that worries me."

Arianna looked at him, confused.

"Really? Who is it that you do not trust?"

"I would rather not say right now. It may be best for me to keep a close eye on them and see how this plays out."

Arianna knew it was best not to argue with Adasser in regards to safety issues. If he had a reason to not tell her why he didn't trust the wizards, then he would tell her in time. However, it would weigh on her mind until he did tell her.

The group finished up their breakfast and were beginning to clean up their camp site when they heard a loud whistle from right outside of the forest. Tanelia looked over to see where it had come from and saw Cassidy and the twins standing on the outskirts of the forest, trying to catch a glimpse of the four travelers. She rolled her eyes and groaned.

"They are here. They are early. It's a good thing the princess didn't sleep in again today."

Arianna sighed. She was exhausted from the lack of sleep

from the night before, coupled with the solidification of what the discovery of the dagger meant. She was growing rather grouchy this morning. She was feeling the weight of this enormous task, and the elf's constant throwing of jabs her way was wearing her patience.

"Can you please refrain from insulting me for *one day*?"

Tanelia shrugged.

"No, don't just shrug your shoulders at me, Tanelia. I have shown you nothing but respect, yet, you seem to think nothing of looking down on me over and over. I'm growing very tired of this attitude. I am exhausted. I have just had the fate of my entire realm thrust upon my shoulders. I don't need some snooty elf adding to the stress level at this point. So, just STOP!"

Arianna's outburst took everyone, including herself, by surprise. She hadn't known that this much irritation had built up inside of her, but, it felt pretty good to just get it out.

Tanelia watched Arianna's outburst with a somewhat confused look.

"Are you finished?"

"Perhaps."

"Good. Now that that is out of your system, let's start this journey so that we can find this wizard and go home."

Arianna threw her hands up and stomped away from the group and made her way to the tree line.

Adasser caught up to her and stopped her from leaving.

"Arianna, I apologize for Tanelia. Her…humor…is somewhat lacking in taste. I can say, honestly, that she has grown quite fond of you."

"Well, she has a funny way of showing it."

"I do not think that her intention was to offend you in any way. Tanelia is tough. She exhibits her affections differently. I am not trying to excuse her behavior. I am simply trying to explain to you that she does care about you."

"Thank you, Adasser, for the inner workings of Tanelia's mind. I am just sick and tired of being used as her verbal punching bag. I didn't ask for any of this. This was all put upon my shoulders. I have had minimal training to do what I am supposed to do and while I am dealing with that, I have to listen to Ellavorn's jealous ex-girlfriend throw insults my way. I don't need that added to my stress level. If she can't show me the same respect that I show her, I would rather her not speak to me at all."

Arianna brushed past Adasser and marched her way to the tree line where Cassidy, Cecilia and, surprisingly, Sumner were all waiting. Cecilia looked excited to be going on the journey. Sumner looked like his blood was boiling over. He was so angry to be going. Cassidy wore a look of indifference on his face, but there was something just beneath the surface that hinted that he was planning on enjoying this trip more than he let on.

Chapter 18

"Trouble in the ranks, Your Highness?" Cassidy had a look of amusement on his face.

"We are just having an argument. It will be fine."

"You were out late last night, enjoying the company of your new dragon, I take it?"

"Yes, Améthystos and I were getting better acquainted."

"And the Elven Prince, he and his dragon were getting along as well?"

Arianna's eyes snapped up to meet Cassidy's. "You know already?"

"Of course I know. They are – were – my dragons. I have known them since they were hatchlings. I had a feeling that Zafeíri would bind himself to your partner. He and Améthystos are bonded. They would not wish to be parted."

Arianna nodded. "I know they are bonded. However, Ellavorn and I are not. At one time, yes, but we are no longer together."

Cassidy's eyebrows knitted in surprise. "I would never have known that you were not an item. You seem very – close."

Arianna smiled a small, sad smile. "It is a long story."

"Perhaps you could tell it to me on our journey. If you are so inclined."

"Perhaps after our journey is completed I will tell you."

"I hope that we survive so that I can hear your story."

"What do you mean by that?"

"I know of the prophecy. I know what you are destined to do. I just didn't realize that you would take my dragons with you."

Arianna heard the bells tinkling in her ears again. "Do not tell him anything, child. He does not know that I was destined to be bound to you. It is urgent that he must not know."

"It was never my intention to insult you or to lure your dragons away, Cassidy. I hope that you believe that. I hope that it will not lead to any distrust between us. I would like for us to be able to trust one another, especially since we will be traveling together for the next few days."

Cassidy seemed to mull the idea over.

"Perhaps we may be able to come to an agreement at some point. For now, we should get moving. It looks like your friends have decided to join us and we have a long journey ahead."

Arianna turned and saw Tanelia, Adasser and Ellavorn

emerging from the woods and walking towards her. She was exhausted and didn't feel up to arguing anymore, so she stayed quiet as they approached. Ellavorn looked to be as tired as she was. He approached her.

"I heard your argument with Tanelia."

Arianna nodded, not sure of where he was going with the conversation.

"Adasser and I had a talk with her after you stomped off."

Arianna looked up at him with a neutral expression.

"Arianna, you have every right to be annoyed with her. She is tenacious when it comes to you. I would be lying if I said I didn't know why because I do. You do know that she cares for you, don't you?"

"Ellavorn, I don't know what to believe. One minute, it feels like she's warming up to me, and the next, she is acting as though she hates me again."

Ellavorn nodded. "I know. Her feelings are conflicted. She cares for you very much. She has admitted that to all of us. She still holds on to the prejudices that she has held on to for her entire life. It isn't right. I know this. Even she knows it. She is trying. She is unsure of how to act around you as well. Your situation is very unique. It will be difficult for many elves to comprehend."

"Adasser and you seem to be perfectly fine with me."

Ellavorn chuckled. "Well, our situations are different. Adasser is in love with your grandmother. I am in love with you."

Arianna froze for a moment, taking in the words that he had just said.

"You are or you were?"

Ellavorn smiled and put his arms around her waist.

"Do you need to be hit over the head with a brick? I was, I am and I always will be, Arianna. I would even join a band of pirates for you."

They both laughed a little laugh and Arianna looked up at him her eyes a little misty, that day in the Glenn seems so long ago, and yet, it was merely a few months that had passed. So much had happened in that time. She felt the guilt from pushing Ellavorn away creeping in again.

"I am truly sorry for hurting you, Ellavorn. I don't know why I pushed you away so hard. I never blamed you for my mother's death. I am so sorry for the awful things that I said that day. I will regret each word until my dying day."

Ellavorn pulled her in closer until she was leaning against him, her head on his chest. He leaned down and kissed the top of her head.

"You were forgiven the moment you said them. As I said, I love you."

"I love you too, Ellavorn."

"Good. When we get back and defeat this creature, can we possibly have that wedding that we were supposed to have?"

Arianna laughed again.

"I think that would be a great idea."

A voice came from behind them.

"Have the lovebirds made amends now?" Tanelia sounded bored.

Arianna grudgingly pulled away from Ellavorn's embrace, missing the feeling of him immediately. She rolled her eyes at the intrusion.

"Yes, we have."

"Good." Her voice dropped into a remorseful tone. "Will I be honored with an invitation?"

Arianna looked at Tanelia for the first time since she had walked over. The elf, usually so proud and strong, looked sad and defeated. Arianna's heart melted a little. Ellavorn excused himself to give them a moment to talk and to help prepare for the journey.

"Arianna, I am sorry for my actions and how they made you

feel. I can understand why you would be frustrated with me and how my words and actions would hurt you. It was never my intention to make you feel that way. I care about you immensely. I have never truly had a friend before. Adasser is more of a father figure to me and Ellavorn, well, you know the history there. I just am unsure of how to navigate this friendship thing."

Arianna sensed the sincerity in her voice. "You've never had a friend before?"

Tanelia sighed. "There is no time for friendships in my line of work. We form a comradery of sorts being in the ranks together for so long, but I would not call it a friendship, not like you humans have."

"Thank you and I accept your apology, Tanelia. I will try to remember that you are learning the magic of friendship as we go and try to have more patience with you as we go. However, can you not make disparaging comments to me first thing after I awaken?"

"I will keep that in mind and make an effort to respect that."

"Thank you. Oh, Tanelia,"

"Yes?"

"I would be devastated if you did not attend the wedding."

Tanelia smiled an actual smile.

"Woah, is that a real smile I see?"

The smile instantly disappeared and Tanelia turned to walk back to the others to prepare to leave.

"Don't push your luck."

Arianna laughed out loud and caught up to her and they walked over to the rest of the group together.

Chapter 19

The group gathered outside of the dragon pen. Améthystos and Zafeíri walked over to Arianna and Ellavorn and the tinkling bells rang in Arianna's ears again.

"Two more dragons will be bonding themselves to the elves."

Arianna's eyes widened and snapped to Adasser and Tanelia.

"Do not tell them, child. They will run."

"They sure will. They do not trust dragons."

"I am aware. Roumpini has informed us of your run-in in the forest. Although, I believe that he has embellished it a bit. He has a flair for the dramatic."

Arianna giggled.

"Can dragons be dramatic?"

Améthystos rolled her eyes.

"I never believed it until he was born."

"But, he seems like a big puppy!"

Améthystos snorted.

"A drama seeking puppy! He tramples Keandra's flowers."

"We witnessed that."

"On purpose," Améthystos was started to sound exasperated by Roumpini's antics.

Arianna laughed.

"Does he really do it on purpose?"

"Every time. He thinks it is funny to see her get so hopping mad. One of these days, she is going to make him pay for it."

Arianna laughed again.

"Will he be joining us on the journey?"

Améthystos sighed.

"Yes, Cecilia will be riding him. He loves Cecilia. She spoils him rotten."

"But, his wing. He was injured by the arrow."

"I keep forgetting that you have a lot to learn, child. Dragon's wounds heal quickly. Our blood not only heals humans, but ourselves too."

"I never thought of that. Why does dragon's blood heal so quickly?"

"It is the magic in us. We don't really know why it has such healing powers, but it heals better than even your partner does."

Arianna blushed.

"Ellavorn asked me to marry him again last night."

Améthystos laughed.

"I know, and you accepted."

"I did. Am I wrong to accept his proposal?"

"No, child, you love him and you have for a very long time."

"I know. I broke his heart once, and then I broke someone else's heart as well."

Cassidy called everyone together.

"I will tell you the story while we are traveling."

"I look forward to that, child."

"Now, those of us who are not bonded to a dragon will choose which dragons to ride to our destination."

He shot Arianna and Ellavorn accusing looks.

"The dragons know their way to my father's house. They have all made the journey before. Trust the dragon that you are riding. We will land a few times to eat and let them rest their wings. We will make camp about half way through the journey. It will take us the better part of the next two days before we arrive."

There was a rumbling sound behind them and everyone turned to see what was happening. Roumpini was galloping towards the group with a turquoise colored and an aquamarine colored dragon right at his heels. Cassidy looked confused until he realized the two other dragons were headed straight towards Adasser and Tanelia. Roumpini, towards the twins.

"Oh, no, no, no, not you two as well!"

The dragons skidded to a stop in front of the elves. The turquoise one, who seemed to be a water dragon, judging from the water dripping from his mouth, stopped in front of Adasser. The aquamarine one, who seemed to be an ice dragon, judging by the icicles that were dangling from her chin, stopped in front of Tanelia.

Cassidy started running towards them, waving his hands in a futile effort to shoo them back into the pasture as the dragons started to do the bonding ritual in what seemed to be fast forward as the motions were a lot faster than when Améthystos and Zafeíri bonded themselves to Arianna and Ellavorn.

Améthystos started laughing again as Cassidy fumed while the two dragons laid their heads at Adasser's and Tanelia's feet.

"He is *very* unhappy right now. He does not like that we are leaving him."

"Améthystos, I know that your destiny is tied to mine and that Zafeíri is following you, but why the other two?"

"We all want to join in this fight with you, child. We all see the light that you bring to the world and the purity of your heart. We need that to stay. We want to help in this war."

She sighed.

"I was hoping that it would not be those two that chose to bond to the other elves. They are Roumpini's brother, Tourkouáz, and sister, Akouamarínis, and they are as rambunctious as he is."

Arianna bit her lip hard to keep from laughing as she pictured Tanelia riding the rambunctious dragon for the next two days. All of the sudden, she was very much looking forward to this journey.

The dragons were still in the finished position, waiting for Adasser and Tanelia to touch their heads. Arianna was debating saying anything when Cassidy growled out,

"Well, go on then, touch their heads. You have to touch their heads to accept them. They want to go with you."

The elves looked terrified, which amused Arianna even more. She tried to make herself look busy, preparing to climb onto Améthystos, but was failing miserably, at hiding the fact that she was watching every move they all made and trying not to laugh at the elves' faces. Luckily, Cassidy didn't notice her because he was too busy trying to get the elves to complete the bonding ritual.

"You have to touch them in order to seal the bond."

Tanelia gave him a disturbed look.

"No way, I am *not* bonding myself to a *dragon*."

Adasser hesitantly reached out his hand while Tanelia looked on incredulously.

"What are you doing?"

"We have to, Tanelia."

His hand made contact with the dragon's head and he looked shocked as the dragon's thoughts rushed into his head. Tourkouáz must have been talking a mile a minute because Adasser looked completely overwhelmed almost immediately. Arianna stifled another laugh and turned her eyes to Tanelia, who was still refusing to touch the dragon. She walked over to her friend.

"Tanelia, you have to touch her head. These dragons are the only way we stand a chance in winning this war. They want to help and, quite frankly, we need them. Please, put your pride away and touch her head."

Tanelia gave Arianna an uneasy look, still unsure of the dragons. She put out her hand and lightly touched Akouamarínis's

159

head. Her thoughts must have invaded Tanelia's brain quickly as well because she gave Arianna a murderous look.

"Great, I get the dragon that won't shut up."

Akouamarínis heard that and snorted, changing the earth beneath Tanelia to turn to ice and making the elf fall, once again, on her rear end. Tanelia gave a frustrated sigh and looked at the dragon that she had just bonded herself to.

"Listen, just because we did this ritual thing, it doesn't mean I have to like it. You're a dragon. You're dangerous. I don't trust you."

Akouamarínis threw her head up in the air as if she was saying, "Well, fine then, be that way, but you're stuck with me."

"Tanelia, try being nice to her. It will make things much easier for both of you."

She held up her hand for Akouamarínis to lower her head. When she did, she stroked her head and whispered to her, "I know Tanelia is tough. She hated me too. Give her some time. She will warm up to you in her own way. Thank you for joining our fight. We need you more than you will ever know."

Akouamarínis closed her eyes for a moment as if to say, "You're welcome."

Arianna turned to look at Tanelia again and found the elf

glaring at her. She bent and whispered in Arianna's ear, "I will *not* warm up to a dragon."

Arianna smirked and said, "We shall see. Remember, you said that about a human too and now look at us. I'm your new best friend."

"I told you not to push your luck."

Arianna laughed and went back to Améthystos.

Cassidy seemed to have recovered from his outrage of two more of his dragons pledging themselves to outsiders who were taking them away. He had gone into the pen and selected a beautiful dark blue dragon, who looked less than thrilled that he was selected to take this journey.

As Cassidy approached the group, he announced,

"Everyone please mount your dragons so that we can be on our way. I would like to get this journey over with."

The group climbed aboard the dragons. Cecilia and Sumner had both climbed aboard Roumpini. The dragons all flapped their wings and one by one, they took off into the sky.

Arianna heard Tanelia scream as the ground got smaller and smaller beneath them and she outright laughed so hard that she almost slipped off of Améthystos.

"Careful, child. Do not laugh so much at the discomfort of

others, or you may experience even more so than they do."

Arianna stopped laughing, which made Améthystos laugh her tinkling bells again.

"Now, child, tell me the story of your other broken engagement."

Arianna sighed and began recounting her story of Ellavorn, Joshua and the mess that she had found herself in.

Chapter 20

A few hours later, Arianna finished up her story of her two broken engagements, the murder of her parents, the Dark Figure, finding her powers and the rest of her journey so far.

"That is quite the journey, child."

"Améthystos, I thought that you could read my thoughts. Could you not see those things?"

"Child, there are things that we know are private. We do not pry into your mind without your permission. We just ask that you afford that same courtesy to us."

"You have my word. I would never intrude into your private thoughts."

"I know that you wouldn't."

"Am I doing the right thing by accepting his second proposal?"

"What does your heart say, child?"

"My heart says yes."

"What does your mind say, child?"

Arianna was confused.

"My mind says yes."

"Now, the most important one, child. What does your gut say?"

"My gut?"

"Yes, child, your gut."

Arianna paused.

"My gut, and every other part of me says yes."

Améthystos smiled.

"There is your answer."

"Why so many questions?"

"Well, your brain is a liar. Your heart, well, the heart is an idiot. Your gut, however, your gut never lies. That is your intuition. However, when all three align, then you know that it is the absolute right thing."

"I know that it is the right thing, Améthystos, but I am scared. I've never been so scared in my life. Not just about Ellavorn, but everything."

"One would never know how scared you are by watching you. I know that you are, child. What you are facing is a scary fate. You have many behind you as you fight this battle. Ultimately, it will be your final battle to fight, but you will have many standing with you."

"Thank you, Améthystos. It truly does bring me comfort that I have allies standing with me."

"You will have more than you know coming to your aid. You are loved by many, even more than you know. They will fight for you. This Dark Figure, it does have its allies too. You will face a formidable battle. I cannot tell you the outcome. I do not know. I do know that you will have many behind you because you give them something to believe in."

"That truly means a lot to me, Améthystos."

"I know it does, child. I am glad for it as well. It means that we have a greater chance of winning this battle."

"Améthystos, why does it mean so much to the dragons that we succeed?"

"We want to come home, child. We want to cross back over to Eumetadotos. We wish to be free. The wizards have taken care of us, but we live under their rule. We are not free. We want our freedom like our ancestors had."

"I can understand that. I know that it will be a concern for my people. The dragons that stay pure will always be welcome. I, along with many others, would worry about their hearts being corrupted. If that were to happen, it would be disastrous."

"I agree with you, child. It is something that we would have to watch carefully. I would not allow anything to happen to jeopardize your trust."

"Thank you, Améthystos. It is definitely something that we will discuss when all of this is over."

"Thank you, child. We will be landing in a moment. We are approaching the first resting point."

Arianna smiled, wondering how Adasser and Tanelia were feeling after their first journey with their newly bonded dragons. She hoped that they were warming up to this development. She was also worried about what Cassidy and the twins were feeling about the situation.

Chapter 21

As Améthystos landed, Arianna slid down off of her back, looking for the rest of the group. She saw Adasser, looking pale, but now as pale as when he rode Améthystos the night prior. She figured that was an improvement. She saw Ellavorn, who looked to still be in deep conversation with Zafeíri. Tanelia, however, she couldn't find at first. Akouamarínis was there, wings raised, but Tanelia was nowhere to be seen. Arianna began to worry that she had fallen off during the journey.

Améthystos's laugh tinkled in her ears again.

"Akouamarínis would never allow that to happen. Remember, they are bonded. If something happens to Tanelia, it would not be good for her. They are probably talking. She will be here soon."

As Améthystos finished her sentence, Akouamarínis lowered her wings and Tanelia slid down, looking as dangerous as ever. Arianna wondered what was on her mind so she began to walk over to her.

"Tanelia, how was your flight? Are you ok?"

"Arianna, does your dragon speak to you? Like, in your mind?"

"Yes."

"Mine NEVER. SHUTS. UP."

Arianna began to laugh hysterically.

"It isn't funny. She just keeps talking and talking. There was not a moment's peace through the whole journey. How do I make it stop?"

Arianna composed herself.

"Have you asked her to stop?"

"I *couldn't*! She didn't give me a chance."

Arianna burst out laughing again.

"You realize I am still armed, correct?"

Arianna stopped laughing immediately.

"Sorry. I got carried away. I just didn't think that the mighty Tanelia would ever not get her way, especially against a chatty dragon."

"It's a *dragon*. What am I going to do?"

"Tanelia, did Akouamarínis tell you anything about dragons?"

"Arianna, that dragon chattered the entire way here. She chattered about which dragon she had a dragon crush on. She chattered about how Roumpini crushed the stupid flowers. She chattered about everything that came into her dragon head. However, she did not tell me anything of importance."

Arianna bit her lip while looking to where she knew Tanelia kept her daggers to keep from laughing again.

"Tanelia, trust her. You have to let your guard down for her."

"She's a *dragon*! How can I trust her? She could turn on us at any moment!"

"No, she can't!"

"Did I mention that she is a *dragon*?"

"Tanelia, she can't turn on you. She has bonded herself to you."

"Yeah, and?"

"When she bonded herself to you, she linked herself to you. If something happens to you, it affects her. If you die, she dies."

Tanelia paled.

"What if she dies?"

"It won't affect you. There have been dragons that have bonded themselves, but whoever they bonded to, they did not suffer at all when those dragons died."

"How do you know all of this, Arianna?"

"Améthystos told me."

"Why did you get the dragon that spills the important information and I get the idle chit chat gossip queen?"

Arianna laughed again. This time, Tanelia joined in.

"Talk to her, Tanelia. Tell her you need a little bit of quiet. Communicate with her."

Tanelia sneered in Akouamarínis's direction.

"If I can get a word in edgewise."

Let's go see what we can do.

"Do we have to?"

Arianna laughed. "Yes."

They turned and walked towards Akouamarínis, who looked excited to see Tanelia coming back towards her. Tanelia groaned and rolled her eyes. Arianna assumed, correctly, that Akouamarínis had started chattering away again.

Arianna stepped forward and held her hand up to stroke Akouamarínis's leg. Akouamarínis lowered her head and Arianna began to stroke her nose. Akouamarínis nuzzled her hand.

"Akouamarínis, I know that you are excited to have bonded

yourself to Tanelia. I know you want to tell her all about yourself. Tanelia, however, needs a little time to process everything. Can you fill her in on some of the perks of being bonded to dragons?"

Akouamarínis nodded her head.

"She said she can do that," Tanelia said.

Arianna leaned in and whispered into Akouamarínis's ear, "She's kind of stuffy too. She doesn't like a lot of small talk. Trust me, I know. She values some quiet time. Are you ok with that?"

"Arianna, what did you say to her? She's *laughing*!"

"I just told her that you like some quite time, that's all," Arianna said as she winked at Akouamarínis.

The dragon winked back and turned towards Tanelia and lowered her head again, as if to apologize to her for talking her ears off on the journey.

Tanelia hesitantly reached out her hand to pet Akouamarínis, who nuzzled her nose into her hand. Tanelia smiled a half smile.

"Ok, dragon, we can work on this."

"Tanelia, use her name."

Tanelia sighed, annoyed, and rolled her eyes. "Fine. Akouamarínis, we can work on this."

Arianna laughed and went to find Adasser to check on him.

Chapter 22

Arianna found Adasser sitting on the ground with Tourkouáz laying curled around him, almost like a nest. They seemed to be talking as she approached. She stepped on a twig and it snapped, alerting Adasser that someone was near. He turned his head quickly to see if there was any danger. When he saw Arianna, he smiled and motioned for her to join them.

"I was worried about how you were feeling after the trip."

Adasser smiled. "I appreciate that. Tourkouáz took good care of me and made sure that the ride wasn't too…intense. We were able to speak to each other. Did you know that we can read each other's thoughts?"

Arianna laughed. "Yes, I've been speaking with Améthystos a lot. Dragons are quite intelligent."

"They truly are. It is remarkable. I never knew that these things were possible."

"Well, it's only if you are bonded that the link forms. I cannot hear what the two of you are saying."

"I wish I had known sooner. It would have come in handy back then."

Arianna reached out and placed her hand on Adasser's shoulder.

"There is no way that you or anyone could have known. The dragons of long ago had already turned. They would not have bonded themselves to anyone unless they carried the same things in their own hearts. It is part of the connection."

Adasser thought for a moment. "So, what you are saying is that the dragons of long ago were, in fact, as dangerous as we believed them to be?"

"Yes, Adasser, that is correct. Améthystos agrees that a turned dragon is dangerous and should be slain. As much as it hurts the rest of them to lose their kin, they understand the dangers."

Tourkouáz snorted in agreement.

"He agrees with you. He has assured me on our journey that he does not hold any grudges towards me or against anyone who took part in the slaying of the dragons. He understands that they had turned and that it was what needed to happen. It was a very interesting conversation."

Arianna smiled. "I'm glad that your conversation with Tourkouáz went a lot better than Tanelia's conversation with Akouamarínis."

Adasser looked confused. "Did they not form the bond? Do they not get along?"

Arianna laughed again. "Well, apparently Akouamarínis likes to talk, and by talk, I mean gossip."

Tourkouáz raised his head with a look in his eyes that seemed to question her.

"Tourkouáz wants to know what she said."

"I don't know exactly, but, apparently, it was a lot of idle chit chat, and Tanelia does not enjoy that."

Tourkouáz looked annoyed.

"He is not happy with Akouamarínis right now. The dragons were supposed to give us information about the bond that we share, not gossip like children. Arianna, I have gotten the impression that this bond is very sacred."

"Adasser, this is probably the most sacred bond that they can form, aside from their mates. It is not something that they have taken lightly. They usually do not form these bonds and link their life spans with another living being."

"He is very excitable, yet, very wise."

Adasser reached out and stroked Tourkouáz's neck. The dragon leaned into his hand as if it brought him comfort.

"I am glad that you are enjoying the bonds that you have all formed with my dragons," Cassidy's voice carried over to them.

"Hello, Cassidy, how was your journey? Are the twins ok as well?"

Cassidy waved his hand as though he were brushing off Arianna's concern.

"Yes, yes, this is a journey that we take often enough. We are used to the flying. I was coming to check on you and your companions and see how you are taking to being bonded to dragons. The elves did not seem to take that news well."

Adasser stood up.

"They are remarkable creatures. I never knew that all of this was possible."

"They are quite extraordinary. It is a shame that the dragons of old never knew kindness, only hatred."

"The dragons of old never cared to known kindness. They were evil by the time they came into contact with us. They only knew greed. If things had been different, and we had known how to prevent them from turning, things would possibly have been different."

Cassidy looked uncertain.

"I don't know so much about that. But, now is not a time for what ifs. We can only dwell on what is."

"Agreed."

"What I want to know is that these dragons that I have raised from hatchlings will be safe when they cross realms back to Eumetadotos. They may have bonded to you all, but I do care what happens to them. They are my children, in a certain aspect. I care for them all very much."

Arianna stood up.

"Cassidy, you have my word that no harm will come to these dragons when we go back. I cannot guarantee anyone's safety when we are in battle, and we will go into battle at some point. However, when we cross realms, I guarantee that no harm will come to them."

Cassidy looked uncertain.

"I will have to trust you on this matter. As much as I do not wish to."

"Trust is all that we have at this point. I know that you care for them. I do too. I will do everything I can to protect them. Once we enter into battle with the Dark Figure, however, I will not be able to protect them all."

"Understood. I do not the like the idea of them going to battle. I do not like that idea in the least."

"I don't like the idea of any of us going into battle. I did not choose to be in this situation. It was forced on all of us. The dragons want to help. That is why they chose to bond themselves to us. I assure you that we did not coerce them in any way."

Cassidy's expression softened for a moment.

"I do not doubt that they would want to help. I feel as though they are ready to return to Eumetadotos."

Cassidy sat facing Adasser and Arianna sat again next to Adasser. Cassidy put his head in his hands. His brown eyes softened and were misty as he spoke.

"It is hard for me to let go. They are like my children. I have helped raise them since they hatched from their eggs. Améthystos and Zafeíri, they have three more eggs in the pyre. I do not wish for them to not know their parents. I am worried."

Arianna's heart softened.

"I understand, Cassidy. I know that this must be very hard on you. I cannot imagine how you must feel, being put in this position. I assure you that we will do everything in our power to keep them all safe."

"I will hold you to that."

Arianna smiled. "You have my word."

"Now that this has been settled, let us start a fire and find something to eat. We should move again soon. We shall fly until evening and then stop for the night."

Cassidy walked away and Adasser waited until he was out of ear shot.

"Do you think that we should trust him?"

Arianna looked her grandfather in the eyes and said, "We don't have any other choice."

Chapter 23

The group gathered firewood and made a fire to make food to eat before beginning the next leg of their journey for the day. Cassidy, Cecilia and Sumner stayed together while Arianna, Adasser, Ellavorn and Tanelia formed their own group. Both groups eyeing the other, suspicious of each other.

When they had all eaten and everything was cleaned up, Cassidy announced that it was time to leave. They all started towards their dragons. However, Arianna caught up to Cassidy and asked to speak with him.

"Cassidy, I understand that you don't trust us, and I understand why you do not. But, please understand that we are not here to harm you in any way. We, or at least I, desire to make amends and, hopefully, form an alliance with you. Please know that I do not agree with my ancestors in their decisions. I would like to reverse those rulings and invite you back."

"Your highness – "

"Arianna, please."

"Your highness, we do not wish to return to Eumetadotos. We have a life here with our dragons, several of which we are losing because of your little trip. I understand you need to meet with my father, and I am willing to take you there, however, I do not wish to form an alliance with you or your elven friends. I will take you where you need to go and that will be the end of our time together."

Cassidy turned and marched away from Arianna, who was left smirking at his back. This wasn't the first time that someone had refused her friendship, and she had a feeling, it wouldn't be the last.

Arianna turned and went to Améthystos, who gave her a suspicious look.

"Child, do not try to befriend him. He will not see reason. It is futile to even try. Besides, he cannot help you. He is bound. A bound wizard is of no use to anyone."

"Améthystos, with all due respect, I don't believe that. There is not a single entity alive that is no use to anyone. Besides, I have a feeling that there is more to Cassidy's story than what is being told."

"Child, I would know. The dragon would have registered this in his memory. We would all have access to this information."

"Do even the turned dragons register what they know?"

Améthystos thought for a second, scanning her memory for anything from any turned dragons in the past.

"It seems that they do not. I have no recollection of those dragons once they turned."

"Then maybe there is something more to this."

"The dragon would not have turned if Cassidy did not embrace evil."

"Améthystos, tell me more about Cassidy before he was bound."

"Cassidy was reckless with his magic. He would treat it as a toy. Always using it for even the most mundane actions. He grew careless and it started backfiring on him. You see, a wizard's magic does not come from within as your power does. Magic is different. It is a learned ability that draws from Nature. Your power is within you, so it will exhaust you as opposed to your surroundings."

"So what I have is not magic?"

"No, child. You have a distinct power inside of you. You were born with it. It may not have been revealed to you until later, but it was always inside of you. Magic is quite different. A wizard needs to learn how to use it. There is training from the time that they are children. Their magic pulls from the elements of Nature."

"So, their magic isn't natural like Elven Powers are?"

"No, it isn't. It is a learned ability."

"So, can anyone learn magic?"

"Technically, yes, but to be powerful like this family is, you need the pedigree that they carry."

"Does Keandra do a lot of magic?"

"She does some. Keandra is more cautious with her magic. She saw what happened to Cassidy. It near drove her to leave. She is still not happy with him, and rightfully so. Cassidy is now bound and has been for several years. We all fear that it will drive him mad at any given point. A wizard who cannot practice magic will usually go mad, especially as gifted a wizard as Cassidy is."

"If he is so gifted, then why did they bind him? Why did they not try to bring him back from the evil?"

"He started to embrace the evil. Once a wizard embraces the evil, they get obsessed with power. Magus made the decision to bind him. It was one of the hardest decisions he ever had to make. It broke his heart to have to do that to his own son."

"Is it possible to undo what has been done?"

"I do not recommend that. If he is unbound, the evil will take over him again. It could be catastrophic."

"So, tell me more about what happened to Cassidy."

"As I said, Cassidy was abusing his magical abilities. He was taking too much from Nature and Nature started to push back. When he had made a campfire, he would try to summon water from the air to put it out and it would result in thunderstorms that lasted a week. He would try to control the wind, only to have a tornado form and destroy trees in the forest. Things like that. Magus saw all of this happening and took action before he lost complete control."

"Why would Nature push back so hard?"

"Because it was trying to restore balance."

"But, he wasn't taking enough to bring on such drastic consequences."

"When you abuse magic for long enough, it distorts the balance too much and it needs to be righted. Nature will do what it needs to do to restore that balance."

Arianna still seemed suspicious of the story, but she could see that there was no changing Améthystos's mind about Cassidy, so she decided to drop the subject.

Améthystos's voice rang in her ears again, "It is time to descend and rest for the night."

Arianna decided that she was going to try and make friends

with the wizards tonight. She knew that Sumner would be the toughest one to get through to, and she already tried to befriend Cassidy to no avail. So, she set her sights on Cecilia for the time being.

"Don't get your hopes up, child."

Arianna snapped to attention.

"Améthystos, I don't think I will ever get used to you being in my head."

The tinkling laugh filled her ears again as they landed.

Chapter 24

The dragons landed one by one and the travelers dismounted. Arianna found Cassidy.

"Where do you want us to set up camp?"

He pointed to the tree line to the right. "There is a place over in the trees there that we usually use for cover. The dragons will conceal themselves. They know what to do."

Arianna nodded and went to gather Adasser, Ellavorn and Tanelia. When she found them, she showed them where to set up camp. They put up the tents and started to gather wood for a fire when they noticed that the wizards hadn't joined them. Arianna and Ellavorn went to look for them while Adasser and Tanelia gathered more wood.

"They don't trust us, Ellavorn, and rightfully so."

"Arianna, we did nothing to betray any trust."

"We haven't done anything to earn it either. Since we've been here, four of their dragons have pledged themselves to us. That is four of their dragons that will not be returning with them. They will need to come back to Eumetadotos with us."

"I understand that, but we did not ask them to pledge themselves to us. They did that of their own accord."

"I know this. But, they have raised these dragons since they were hatchlings. Améthystos and Zafeíri, they have three eggs in that pyre that we saw. They are leaving their children behind to fight with us. There is no guarantee that they will survive this fight. I don't blame the wizards for being angry or distrustful of us."

"Arianna, we need all of the help that we can get in this battle. It is why we are here."

"Oh, Ellavorn, I know. I am grateful that the dragons wish to help us in our plight. I truly am. But, I do empathize with Cassidy, Cecilia and Sumner. They are losing their family members, possibly for good."

Ellavorn sighed. "We could bring them to visit, or they can visit us."

"Depending on if we win this battle, and if they even wish to visit."

Ellavorn stepped in front of Arianna, facing her and reached out, taking hold of her arms.

"Do not speak like that. We are going to win this battle. We are going to save our kingdom and our entire realm. We have to."

Arianna smiled.

"I hope so. I just feel so scared and unprepared for this. I don't know if I am capable of winning this."

Ellavorn pulled her into a warm embrace and said to her,

"You will fight and you will win. I have never seen you fail. I know for a fact that you would not stop at anything but winning the most important task that faces you."

"I will not give up easily. I will not just allow some coward who cannot show their face take over my kingdom. I will fight to the end. I just fear that, even if I win, I will lose."

"What do you mean?" Ellavorn was confused.

"I mean, we have been gone for weeks now. I worry about what is happening in Eumetadotos. I don't know what is happening with Abigail or Joshua or your father or anyone. Is Iron Demon still afflicted with the argós thánatos? Is he still locked in the dungeon? Has the Dark Figure attacked again? Does it even know that I am not there? What will it do if it knows I'm not there? Will it hurt Abigail or the others?"

Ellavorn squeezed her a little tighter.

"Arianna, you cannot be everywhere at once. You are doing what you have to do to protect everyone. They know this. My father is there. He will protect them all. You know that you have the aid of the elves in this, correct?"

"Thank you, Ellavorn. I am still very worried about my friends and my people."

Ellavorn tilted her face to his and smiled a comforting smile.

"This is why I love you, Arianna. You are always thinking of what is best for everyone."

He softly kissed her and she relaxed.

"Thank you, Ellavorn. I love you too. I just wish that we could rewind to a few months ago, back when everything was easy and innocent and promising. I want to go back to when there was no death or hatred or exposed family secrets. I want to go back to that last day in the Glen, back before everything went wrong."

"I know. I wish that we could go back too. I admire how far you have come from that day. You are so strong. You have been handling this extremely well. I know that you have your moments. You are supposed to. Life will always get hard at times. But, I promise you, I will always be there for you when you need me to be. I will be there for you even when you don't need me. Arianna, you are my North Star, my guiding light."

Arianna sighed, "How do you always know how to make me feel better? You always have the right words to say. You have always been there for me, even when I feel like I am about to fall apart and I can't take anymore. Ellavorn, you are my rock that keeps me in place. I love you. I am forever grateful that I get to spend my days with you by my side."

"Are you ok to move forward now?"

Arianna pulled back, keeping her hands locked around his waist, looked up at him, smiled and said, "I am. Let's go find the wizards."

Chapter 25

Arianna and Ellavorn started walking again and soon came across the wizards' camp. They were sitting by the fire, deep in conversation. As soon as they realized that they had company, the conversation stopped. Sumner made a snarling face at the visitors. Cassidy's expression was indifferent and Cecilia looked conflicted, as though she wanted to greet their guests, but something was holding her back.

"Can we help you, Your Highness?" Cassidy spoke up.

"We were just checking in with you all to see how your ride was," Arianna answered, not daring to take any movement forward without an invitation.

Cecilia smiled. Sumner scoffed. Cassidy answered,

"We have made this trip multiple times in the past. We know how to make the trip satisfactory."

"Oh, ok. I was just making sure that everyone is safe."

Sumner scoffed again, and while rolling his eyes said, "Such a wonderful leader you are."

Arianna looked taken aback. She didn't think she could ever get used to the hatred that Sumner felt towards her. She addressed him.

"Sumner, I understand that you feel a great deal of animosity towards my ancestors, and that has trickled down to me as well. I do not wish you any harm, in fact, I would like to try to make reparations for what my ancestors did to yours."

Sumner sneered at her, "As if you could ever undo what they did. Curse your people. I want nothing to do with you or your reparations. I am only here to see to it that you don't steal any more of our dragons."

Arianna narrowed her eyes at Sumner.

"I did not steal your dragons. They pledged themselves to us. They want to help us in this fight. I did not ask them to do anything. I did not even know that dragons still existed anywhere."

"Of course not. Because the people of Eumetadotos just kill or banish anything that they don't like."

Cassidy broke in,

"Sumner! You know that you are wrong on this one. The dragons that were killed back then were not the same as the ones we have now. They had turned. You know this. You cannot fault the people for defending themselves against evil. You *know* that we would do the same here."

Sumner gave his father a look of disgust and stormed off to his tent.

"I apologize for his outburst. Please, excuse me while I go have a chat with my son."

Cassidy walked off to Sumner's tent, leaving Arianna and Ellavorn alone with Cecilia. Arianna saw this as her opportunity to break the ice with the girl. She walked over to where Cecilia sat.

"Is it ok if I sit with you?"

Cecilia looked confused.

"Why?"

"I just wanted to talk with you and get to know you somewhat."

Cecilia looked at Arianna and over to Ellavorn and back to Arianna again.

"Is he going to be chatting too?"

"Possibly. Is it ok if he does?"

"I don't like elves much."

"I know. I can ask him to stay back if you wish."

"I wish."

"Ok. That is fine."

Arianna turned to Ellavorn and asked, "Can you please wait for me over by the trees?"

Ellavorn gave her a suspicious look, but did as he was asked.

"Is it ok if I sit with you now?"

"Ummmm, sure."

Arianna sat down and gathered her thoughts for a moment, trying to figure out what to say to break the ice.

"Cecilia, why does your brother hate me so much? I know that my ancestors banished yours to this realm. I understand that hatred. However, I am trying to make things right again. I would like to be friends with all of you, whether you choose to help us or not."

Cecilia sighed.

"Sumner feels as though we were robbed of our birthright, to become powerful wizards in our native land. We do not have some of the same plants and other things that grow in Eumetadotos that we need for certain spells or potions. He feels as though some of our freedoms with practicing magic were taken away and he harbors that resentment to the extreme."

"I can see the resentment. I've never felt hatred that strong, and I've been on the wrong side of Tanelia!"

Cecilia giggled.

"She seems very—tough?"

"She is. She is very suspicious of humans. A lot of elves are. Elves don't die a natural death, so many of them see this as a weakness. I think that she is coming around, at least I hope so."

"Death is natural. Being immortal is not. Immortality can make you reckless. At least, that is what my grandfather said."

"Is that why you dislike elves? Because you think that they are reckless?"

Cecilia thought for a moment.

"I don't know. I just don't trust any creature that can live forever."

Arianna knew that elves could be killed, but something inside her told her not to divulge that information just yet.

"I understand your thinking. They are quite interesting creatures."

"How so?"

"They are more like humans than they think that they are, yet, some of them tend to hate us for what they perceive as a flaw…our mortality."

"How are they like us? They don't seem like it. They seem a bit…stuck up."

Arianna stifled a giggle.

"Not all elves are stuck up. Take Ellavorn, for example. We are engaged again."

"Again, really?"

"Yes, as I told you the other day, I hastily called off the first engagement, but now that we are reunited after his sojourn with the pirates, we seem to be back on the same path again."

"I thought elves didn't mate with humans? Something about it tainting their bloodlines?"

"Well, that is true. Most elves don't mate with humans. But, we have come to find out recently that he is not the first."

Cecilia's jaw dropped.

"An elf mated with a human?"

"Yes."

"What happened?"

"Well, my mother was born from that union between my grandmother and Adasser."

Cecilia jumped up and squealed at the gossip that she was hearing.

"*That* Adasser?? The one that is here with you?"

Arianna was trying very hard not to break out laughing.

"Yes, Adasser is, apparently, my grandfather."

"Was he king?"

"No. He and my grandmother fell in love and had an affair. She was forced to marry my grandfather, but she was pregnant with my mother already. She didn't know for sure who the father was. No one knew about the affair until recently."

"But, how did they find out?"

Arianna looked at her feet.

"Because my powers showed up."

Cecilia's eyes grew as big as saucers.

"You have powers?"

"Yes."

"Can I see?"

Arianna laughed.

"I am still not in complete control of them. I'm getting better, but I still need more practice."

Cecilia pouted.

Arianna stood and turned around and threw a ball of light at a bush nearby. The bush blew up, making a loud noise and summoning Ellavorn, Cassidy and Sumner back to the fire.

"What happened? Arianna, are you ok?" Ellavorn ran to her side, looking over her for any injuries.

Cassidy and Sumner ran to Cecilia's side, looking her over as well.

"We're fine. Cecilia wanted to see my powers. I was just demonstrating."

Sumner gave his sister a furious look, growled and stormed off again.

Cassidy looked at Arianna in wonder.

"Wait, you have powers? How is that possible? Only elves have powers."

"Father, Adasser is her grandfather!"

Cassidy's eyebrows raised.

"An *elf* mated with a *human*?"

"Yes, Adasser and my grandmother had a love affair before my grandmother married my grandfather. My mother was conceived during that affair."

"Your mother was a half-elf?"

"Yes, but she never knew. She died before we found out. My powers revealed themselves by accident."

"Elves do not mate with humans."

"Well, no, most don't. Adasser did, and Ellavorn and I were engaged before we found out about my heritage."

Cassidy looked at Ellavorn in wonder.

"You were going to mate yourself to a human?"

"I was, and still will," Ellavorn seemed to be a little agitated with being on display.

Cassidy threw his head back and laughed.

"Oh, if grandfather could only hear this story."

"Well, as it turns out, I am not fully human."

"Yes, I am curious to know. How *did* you find that out?"

"I guess we should all sit around the fire and I can tell the story. It is quite long."

The entire group sat around the campfire. Sumner, surprisingly, joined them as well. Arianna hoped that this was a sign of promise that he was warming up to her. Ellavorn, however, seemed to continue to distrust him. Even Cassidy was surprised by his son's willingness to participate in the telling of the story. Arianna began telling the story of how they came to be in this realm.

When Arianna had finished, the wizards had some

questions.

"Arianna, did you ever have any indication that you possessed powers before this incident with this Dark Figure as you call it?" Cassidy was curious.

"No, not that I recall. I always thought that I was an ordinary human."

This elicited a smirk from Cassidy.

"Well, I knew from first glance that you were no ordinary human. Your eyes gave it away."

Arianna nodded. "Yes, you mentioned that you knew of the prophecy. I didn't realize that wizards knew about it. I thought it was only elves that knew."

Cassidy smirked again. "Well, Your Highness, you are not the only one with a backstory. However, that will have to wait for another time. We must get some sleep so that we have the strength to continue our journey tomorrow. Cecilia, Sumner that includes you as well."

"Yes, father."

Cassidy and Sumner turned and started to leave.

Cecilia then turned to Arianna.

"Thank you for telling us your story. It was quite

interesting."

"Thank you for listening. I hope that I am not being too forward with this, but I hope that we can form a friendship and that you would consider coming back with us. We could use all of the help that we can get."

"I will think that over and discuss it with my father and my brother. I do not know that Sumner will ever be on board with it, but I may be able to convince father."

"Thank you, Cecilia. I do appreciate it. We need all of the help that we can get."

"I can't make any promises, Arianna, except that I will try."

"Trying is all that you can do."

Chapter 26

Arianna and Ellavorn started walking back to their campsite, both silent and deep in thought.

"Arianna, do you think that it is wise that you told the wizards so much of what is going on back home?"

"I had to Ellavorn. They needed to know the whole story if we are to earn their trust."

Ellavorn didn't feel reassured by her answer.

"Arianna, I think that you are putting too much faith in the wizards. I do not think that they would agree to come back with us to fight this evil. We may be on our own."

Arianna stopped and turned to face Ellavorn.

"Or we may not. We have to try, Ellavorn. We need all of the help that we can get. I don't know that we will be able to persuade them, but I have to try. My kingdom depends on it. I know that Cassidy hates us already."

"I do not hate you, your highness," Arianna and Ellavorn both jumped at the sound of Cassidy's voice coming from behind a tree. He chuckled at their reactions.

"Always be aware of your surroundings. There is nothing to harm you here with all of the protective spells put in place by all of us. However, you never know what is lurking around dark corners."

Arianna looked curious.

"I thought you went back to sleep."

"Ah, yes, well, I don't exactly sleep well these days," he said as he rubbed his neck. He had a fleeting wistful look on his face, but seemed to snap out of his daze quickly.

"What do you mean that you don't hate us? Your dragons pledged themselves to us. We have to take them with us. I know you can't be happy about that."

Cassidy smiled a small, sad smile.

"Well, no, I am not especially happy that they are leaving. However, I know that they will need to fulfill whatever destinies that they have in this life, whether it is with or without my help. I have raised them since they were hatchlings and to know that they are going to war, and possibly their deaths, it hurts me to know that."

"I do assure you that we will take the best possible care of them. I don't want any of them to come to any harm. However, we do need them in this fight. Just as we need your help, if you would be willing to give it to us."

Cassidy nodded in understanding.

"I cannot commit to that just yet, your Highness. I have to worry about my children as well. They are not quite old enough to be without both of their parents just yet."

With that, Cecilia jumped from behind another tree.

"I wish to fight, Father. We can help them!"

"Cecilia! You were told to go to bed. What are you doing out here so late?"

"Probably the same as you, Father. Making sure that our *friends* got back to their tents safely." Everyone present took notice on the emphasis she made on the word friends.

"Your brother will never agree to it."

"My brother is a warty toad who is only happy when he is miserable."

"Cecilia!"

"Ugh! Sorry!" She said, "But, it's true," she mumbled under her breath. Arianna heard it and tried to hide her smile.

"Cecilia, go back to your tent and get some rest. We will discuss this in the morning."

Cecilia made a noise of disgust and turned and stomped back to her tent. Arianna watched the scene unfold and smiled, missing her own father in that moment. She remembered the arguments that she had with him over the years and wished for just one more.

"Your Highness?"

Arianna snapped out of her daydream.

"I am sorry. My mind was somewhere else."

Cassidy nodded. "I was saying that I will walk you the rest of the way back to your tent and so that you can get some rest."

Ellavorn eyed Cassidy suspiciously, but said nothing.

"Do not worry, Your Other Highness, I mean no harm to either of you. I am actually happy to have you here, although it does not seem like I am."

Ellavorn nodded and Arianna began speaking again.

"I understand your hesitation in joining our fight, Cassidy. I will not try to influence you either way. I just want to you believe me when I tell you that I truly did not expect to see dragons, let alone have four of them accompany us back to Eumetadotos."

Cassidy looked at her and smiled again.

"I know it was not your intention. The dragons have made their decision and I need to respect that decision. My ancestors and I have known for a very long time that this may happen. The dragons were never truly happy here. It is not their natural home.

We preserved their bloodlines for as long as we could. We knew that they were destined to return some day, just as we are. I just do not know that this is the time for the wizards to return."

"I understand, Cassidy. I do appreciate your help and I would like to tell you that your family is welcome back to Eumetadotos any time that you would like to return."

Cassidy looked at Arianna, and she swore that there was a tear in his eye.

"Thank you, Your Highness. I will return one day. Maybe not soon, but I will return."

They walked the rest of the way back to the tents in silence and once they got there, Adasser and Tanelia rushed to greet them but stopped short when they realized that Cassidy was walking with their friends.

Cassidy nodded to them, and they eyed him warily.

"It's ok. Cassidy was just walking us back to make sure that we made it back safely."

"We can take care of them from here," Adasser snapped, causing both Arianna and Ellavorn to look at him strangely. It was out of character for Adasser to act protectively over them.

"I understand, the grandfatherly instinct to protect his kin is kicking in," Cassidy taunted.

Adasser growled a very, very low growl at him, which made Cassidy laugh softly.

"It is ok, Adasser, he knows."

Adasser looked surprised.

"Arianna, you told them of your heritage?"

"Yes, I felt that I had to tell them the whole story in case they may want to help."

Adasser scoffed.

"Adasser, we need all of the help that we can get. Now, I think that we should all go back to our tents and get some rest. We have the rest of our journey to complete."

Arianna started off in the direction of her tent, leaving the elves to look after her incredulously. Cassidy, however, laughed out loud.

"You can tell that the lot of you are not used to taking orders from humans." He looked back at Arianna, watching her walk in the direction of her tent, marching on with a purpose.

"Oh, do you three have your hands full."

He walked back in the direction of his side of the camp, laughing.

Chapter 27

Arianna tossed and turned all night, wondering if she did the right thing telling the wizards of her heritage. It was bound to come out at some point, so she didn't understand why Adasser was so concerned. She finally fell asleep, but was awakened by the tinkling voice of Améthystos.

"Come, child. It is time to wake up. We have a journey to complete."

Arianna's eyes flickered open and she got up and left her tent. The elves were sitting around the fire, speaking in hushed tones. When they saw her, they stopped talking.

"Good morning, Arianna, would you like some breakfast?" Adasser asked her, his tone a little on the cold side.

"Please."

He made her a plate and passed it to her and walked off in the direction of the tents to start packing his belongings. Tanelia got up and went to pack her things as well, leaving Ellavorn and Arianna alone.

"They are angry with me?"

"A little. They don't understand why you would tell your

secrets to the wizards. You barely know them."

"Ellavorn, we need to try to win them over. We need help in this fight. They will bring a level of magic that we do not possess. Besides, think of Charlie. When this is all over, he will need someone to tutor him. His powers are strong, you can tell. They may become even stronger with some help from trained wizards."

Ellavorn shook his head.

"We will never understand humans. Give them a little time. They will come around. They always do. They have both grown very fond of you, Arianna. They are worried about you. You hold the key to the success of this fight within you. Without you, we are lost."

"I know this, Ellavorn. I am trying my best to figure this all out. I don't have any sort of guidance here. It is all new to me. I have to follow what my heart is telling me and it is saying that we need to trust the wizards. We need to win them over somehow. We need them."

Ellavorn sighed.

"None of us have the answers. I wish that we did. We do not know how this is going to play out. All I know is that I need you to be safe while fulfilling your destiny."

Arianna smiled.

"I understand. But, you also have to know that being completely safe is not an option for me. I am the one who has to defeat this figure. I have to be in the front lines when we go to battle. I have to be the protector this time."

Ellavorn nodded.

"I know this. I have known for a long time that this is how it would have to be. I will not stand in the way of you fulfilling your destiny, however, I will be right behind you to protect you when I can."

Arianna smiled.

"Thank you. I know that you understand the severity of the situation. But, you have to understand that we need all of the help that we can get."

"I do, Arianna. The others do as well. They just continue to have their suspicions about the wizards. They will come around, I hope."

Adasser and Tanelia appeared, seemingly out of nowhere.

"It is not that we do not support the choices that you are making, Arianna," Adasser started.

"We are concerned about the wizards' intentions. Their family was banished many, many years ago by your family. We do not know how they feel now. And, with the development of the...dragons..." Adasser still looked uneasy at the mention of the dragons.

"We do not know what their plans are to prevent the dragons from leaving with us."

"I assure you, dear elf, that we will not try to cause you any harm, nor will we prevent the dragons from leaving with you. We will not be the reason that any of them come to harm," Cassidy said, appearing from behind the tree line.

"It was not my intention to insult you, Cassidy. Please forgive me. I was just saying that we do not know you well enough to form an educated opinion on what your intentions are."

"Well, Adasser, I, myself, am not entirely sure what my intentions are." He looked over at Arianna and gave a small smile.

"However, I do trust Arianna. She has shown me the willingness to work with me, and has given me her word that she will do everything in her power to protect the dragons. They have made their choice. I will honor it without interference."

Arianna smiled at Cassidy.

"Thank you, Cassidy."

Cassidy nodded again.

"I still cannot give you an answer as to whether my family

will fight with you. I will need to consult with my father in that matter. He will be able to give us the guidance that you seek."

"I understand."

"Now, we need to get our things together and move on. We are not too far from my father's house. It is just up that mountain there," He pointed in the direction that they would be traveling and they all took notice of the mountain that they could not see in the dark of night.

Arianna gasped at the sheer height and the beauty of the majestic, snow covered mountain.

"No worries, Your Highness, the dragons will be able to handle that with ease. We are not going all the way to the top. My father lives about three quarters of the way up. The rest of the journey will be easy."

Arianna smiled and nodded, but she didn't feel so sure.

Chapter 28

The group all met up and climbed onto the dragons. Arianna was a bit quiet as Améthystos took off on the final leg of their journey.

"I hear that you told the wizards of your heritage, child."

Arianna stayed quiet.

"I will not judge you for doing something that you felt you needed to do. I know that you did not spill any of our secrets to them, for which I am grateful. Why are you so quiet today?"

Arianna sighed.

"I think that I made the elves angry by telling the wizards of my heritage. I don't understand why they are so upset with me. It is my story to tell. I was just trying to earn their trust. Améthystos, we need their help. I know that we didn't exactly win any favor when you all pledged yourself to us."

Améthystos gave a little snort of laughter.

"No, they were not happy with that situation. I know that Cassidy has said that he does not blame you, and that he supports us."

"Do you believe him?"

Améthystos sighed.

"I wish to. For all of their flaws, the wizards were good to us. They made sure that we were safe and protected and that we were fed. They have learned much from our kind. Most of which benefits them more that it benefits us."

"Such as the dragon blood having healing qualities?"

"Precisely, child. I know that they would not like to give up on that very quickly."

Arianna smiled.

"I'm sure that it was quite handy to have around. I am curious, though. How did they harvest the blood and how did they come to find out about its healing qualities?"

"They have never harmed us, child. We dragons can be, well, a bit clumsy, especially when we are young. When they would see an open wound, they would collect the blood then. They never cut us to collect it."

"How did they know that it healed them?"

"That came about as an accident. Cassidy was out for a ride one day with my father. When they landed, his footing was poor and both fell to the ground. My father suffered a large, however, minor cut. Cassidy had a deep gash in his arm. Some of my father's blood dripped onto Cassidy's gash by accident, and it started to heal itself almost instantly."

"So, dragons didn't know that your blood could heal humans until that point?"

"No, child. It was a surprise to us all. After that fall, they would keep jars of our blood in the shed in case of emergencies. We have had a shed full of jars for quite a while, especially since Roumpíni can along."

Ariana laughed.

"He is quite…spirited…isn't it?"

Améthystos sighed and shook her head.

"He is quite rambunctious. Most dragons find his exuberance quite annoying."

"He reminds me of a puppy."

"Yes, I can see that. Be quite careful with him, though, child. He may seem harmless, but he is quite strong."

"I am sure that Keandra's flowers think so."

Améthystos laughed.

"Yes, he does like to get under her skin with those flowers. He is quite the scoundrel."

Arianna laughed.

"Do you regret your decision to inform the wizards of your

heritage?"

"I don't know. It seems to have upset the elves. Maybe it wasn't such a great idea."

"I did not ask about the elves. Take them out of the equation. Do you regret informing them of your heritage?"

Arianna thought for a moment.

"No. I do not regret it. I did what I thought I had to do to earn their trust. I felt that letting them know who I truly am would be the first way to do that."

"I have heard that it has worked, child. They are starting to warm up to you, at least Cassidy and Cecilia are. I am afraid that Sumner is a lost cause. I do not think that he will ever come around to your side."

Arianna started to feel hope bloom in her chest.

"Do you think that they will help join the fight?"

"I cannot say for sure, child. Magus would be the one to make the decision to accept your royal pardon. Améthystos."

"Oh, no."

"Is something wrong, child?"

"Yes! Technically, I am no longer the queen."

"What do you mean that you are no longer the queen?"

"Well, when Iron Demon attacked, he was going to kill everyone unless I abdicated the throne to him."

"Please tell me that you didn't."

"I had to. You see, the Dark Figure placed a curse on the position of King and Queen. The Argós Thánatos."

Améthystos gasped.

"The Argós Thánatos has no cure. How are you still alive?"

"Ellavorn's father, Armen, and Adasser concocted an Apokatástasi potion. They made it for me and would give me full doses."

"That is brilliant. Is Iron Demon taking this potion? Is he ruling the kingdom?"

"Well…we tricked him. Once I abdicated, the curse passed on to him. I instructed Armen to give him just enough of the potion to keep him alive, but unconscious. He is laying in a dungeon right now. However, he is the King right now."

"And how were you intending to fix this complication?"

"Well, when we get back, we were going to persuade him to abdicate the position back to me. We would inform him that the position had been cursed and that there is no cure for the ailment, aside from the potion, which will not work forever."

"Is that part true?"

"We don't know for certain. I am now concerned over whether or not the wizards can cross back to Eumetadotos. The ban calls for the King or Queen to issue a pardon. I am no longer the Queen."

"No, child. The ban requires a pardon from your family. You should be fine. You do need to get back to Eumetadotos to have him abdicate the position back to you. The curse is needed to help in this fight."

Arianna was confused.

"How will being cursed help?"

"It isn't the curse so much as the cure for the curse."

"I thought that there was no cure."

"Your betrothed is a healer, is he not?"

"Well, yes."

"Have you had an affliction before?"

"Once, as a child. Ellavorn had healed me before from a strange illness."

"Child, you have been cursed before. He healed you then.

He can do it again now."

"Améthystos, I was cursed as a person. The curse has been placed on the position of King and Queen."

"Yes, but he is a very, very powerful healer. He can fix this."

"I hope that he can. I desperately need his help."

"He can and he will. His love for you knows no boundaries. He will do whatever you ask of him."

"Well, then, let's get to Magus so that we can return home."

Améthystos laughed her tinkling laugh again.

"We are already there."

Arianna looked up to see a homey looking cottage beneath her, white smoke coming from the chimney and a dark blue dragon laying curled up in a ball in the front yard.

The dragons all landed one by one as the door opened and a tall, rail-thin white haired man with a long, white beard with steel-gray eyes, dressed in deep red robes covered in golden stars stepped out.

"Well, it's about time you all showed up," Magus announced in a cheery, yet deep, booming voice.

Chapter 29

Cecilia leapt from Roumpíni and ran to Magus and threw her arms around him.

"Grandfather!"

"Hello, my dear girl. I've missed you."

Sumner walked to his grandfather's side, glaring over at Arianna, Ellavorn, Adasser and Tanelia.

"I see that you are as chipper as ever, Sumner. To what do we owe this ever so pleasant mood today?"

Sumner scowled at his grandfather and turned and went into the house.

"Hello, Father."

Magus took a long look at his son.

"Cassidy, you are looking well."

Cassidy nodded.

"Father, I would like to introduce Queen Arianna, Prince Ellavorn, Adasser and Tanelia. They are from – "

"Eumetadotos."

"Yes, Father. Eumetadotos."

"You are the prophesized child," he said to Arianna.

Arianna looked around at the rest of the party.

"Did *everyone* but me know about the prophecy?"

Magus laughed.

"Your Highness, elves and wizards have exchanged prophesies and knowledge for centuries. Your birth has been foretold for a long, long time."

Arianna sighed, "I just wish that I knew sooner so that I was more prepared."

Magus walked over to her and took a long look at her.

"You are very well prepared. Not completely, but you are learning very quickly. And remember, some things can only be learned by experience alone."

Arianna looked confused.

"What I mean by that, You Highness is that you can train for many, many year, but until you face an actual battle, you do not know what you can accomplish."

"I wish that I did not have to accomplish anything to be honest."

"Well, to achieve anything great, you must accomplish something."

"Most people do not have to accomplish saving an entire realm from certain doom."

Magus gave her a small smile.

"No, Your Highness, they don't. That is what defines the great from the amazing. You are destined for amazing things. You may feel as though you are overwhelmed, but you are meant to do this."

"What if I fail?"

"But, what if you succeed?"

Arianna looked at Magus incredulously.

"What do you mean?"

"You are so worried about failing and what will happen in the aftermath. Have you given any thought as to what will happen if you succeed?"

Arianna was confused by this question.

"Well, if I succeed, life will go back to normal."

Magus laughed.

"Your Highness, life will not go back to the normal that you once knew."

Arianna thought for a moment, realization dawning on her

that once the battle was done, and if she was the victor, that her life would never be the same. Normal for her would be completely redefined. Magus saw the look on her face and started talking again.

"Your life will never be like it was before, but that does not mean that it wouldn't be better. It will just be different."

"I just never thought about it. I guess I just got so caught up on fighting this battle that I never thought of what would happen after that battle."

"That is normal. We all get caught up in the daily happenings and forget that another option is possible. Now, you need to plan what you will do if you succeed?"

Arianna looked confused again. "But, I don't understand why that is important."

Magus's eyes grew large in amazement.

"Your Highness, it is important to focus on what will happen as a result of success so that you have something to aim for in the darkest of moments. And, Your Highness, there will be dark moments. I cannot tell you that there will not be. You are preparing for war."

Arianna's face fell.

"That is the part that I did not want to happen. I don't want to lose anyone."

"That is understandable. We never want to lose anyone we care about. I can see that you are one that cares very deeply. Keep that trait. The world needs that kindness and love. But, you need it shown to you too as well."

Magus looked over to Ellavorn.

"You are her betrothed, am I correct?"

Ellavorn looked confused.

"Yes, I am."

"You need to help her to focus on success."

Adasser stepped forward.

"We have all been a part of Arianna's training."

Magus looked Adasser up and down, raised one eyebrow and said, "You are related to our lovely queen?"

Adasser raised his chin and indignantly looked at Magus.

"I am her grandfather."

"Yes, yes, this is where her elven blood comes in."

"How did you know that?"

Arianna's head whipped around to look at Cassidy, who

seemed as surprised as the rest of them that Magus knew about Arianna's heritage.

Magus shook his head.

"Wizards are known for knowing things. We are quite good at it, actually."

Arianna looked confused.

Magus laughed, "We have the ability to see into the future and all possible outcomes in any choices that are made."

"Is this how you knew we were coming?"

Magus smiled.

"That was part of it. The other one was the fact that Ydátinos was pacing back and forth as if she was waiting for someone."

The group looked over at a beautiful, deep blue dragon who was standing in a fenced in clearing, craning her neck to see who had arrived.

The dragons all began moving over to her and stepped over the fence effortlessly.

Arianna looked at Magus and asked, "Why do you have the fence if the dragons can just step over it?"

Magus shrugged.

"It seemed like the right thing to do at the time."

Arianna turned to look over at Améthystos and the rest of the dragons. Améthystos caught her eye and her sweet voice rang in Arianna's ears.

"Go inside, child. It is safe. Magus will help you to get back to your people and will clear up some concerns you may have. We need our rest out here now."

Arianna looked back at Magus, who smiled at her.

"I see that the dragons have chosen you all. Good, good. Things are happening the way that they should be."

He then turned and went into the house, revealing the huge gold moon on the back of his robe, motioning for the group to follow.

Chapter 30

The group followed Magus into the house, looking around in awe. There were books were lining ever wall and sitting in numerous stacks on the floor, herbs were hanging from the ceiling all over. The windows were covered in red fabric that matched Magus's robes with just a sliver of sunlight streaming through. Arianna's eyes fell on a crystal ball surrounded by crystals in the corner.

Magus followed her gaze and smiled.

"I see you noticed my scrying ball."

Arianna moved closer to the clear ball.

"What does it do?"

"It tells me what is going on when I can't be in certain places."

Arianna looked at him suspiciously.

"Is this how you knew that we were coming?"

"Mmmmmm hmmmm," Magus nodded.

Arianna walked over to the ball and looked through it. The only thing she saw was a distorted vision of Cassidy, who was shifting from one foot to another as though he was nervous about something.

"How does it work?"

Magus smiled, stood next to her and ran his finger down the side of the ball.

"You have to concentrate on what you want to see. It won't work immediately. It takes a lot of practice and hard work."

He covered the ball with a red velvet cloth, which was also covered in stars.

"Come this way." He motioned for them to follow and led them into a sitting room that was full of oversized furniture. Cassidy sighed as he followed him.

"Please, make yourselves at home," Magus indicated to the furniture around the room.

Arianna chose the sofa in the middle of the room. Ellavorn sat down next to her, closely, almost protectively. Arianna smiled at him and put her hand on his arm. He looked at her, smiled, and put his hand over hers.

"Ahhhhh, yes, the Elven Prince who has fallen for a human…or, should I say three-quarter human."

Ellavorn's eyes locked on Magus, his expression was guardedly curious.

"Yes, I know about that too. I keep tabs on the daily gossip in Eumetadotos," Magus smirked.

"So, you spy on us, then?" Ellavorn's stance got a little more defensive.

"Relax, Prince. I do look in to see what is happening. I like to keep up to date on what happens over there so that I could prepare for this particular visit."

Cassidy had moved to the back of the room, leaning on a deep windowsill. He rubbed his face and sighed.

"Yes, Father, we get the point that you can predict the future. I think that our guests may want to discuss what is happening back in Eumetadotos so that they can get back there to finish this war that has been going on."

Magus shot his son a dirty look.

"Patience is still not your virtue, I see."

"Father, they came here for help. Let's just help them so that they can get home. I think that they are anxious to do so."

Magus grunted and turned to Arianna.

"Your Highness, I apologize if I have been an inconvenience to you."

Arianna looked confused.

"You are not an inconvenience to me at all."

Magus turned to Cassidy and smirked as if to say, "Well,

there you go," and turned his back to his son.

"Father, they do not have time to play games. Their kingdom, their entire realm, is in danger. We do not have time to give lessons on fortune telling or anything of such. They need –."

Cassidy's sentence was cut off as Magus snapped his fingers and one of the colorful orbs from the vision Armen had conjured appeared out of nowhere and dropped down on Cassidy's head, breaking open and soaking him. Cassidy's expression turned to one of a murderous rage towards his father as he clenched his jaw shut and stormed out of the room. Magus, however, was doubled over in laughter. Arianna and the Elves looked at each other, none of them sure what to think. Cecilia was the first to speak.

"I don't think my father took that very well, Grandfather."

Magus turned to his granddaughter with a smile on his face, "Your father used to have a sense of humor."

Cecilia shook her head and started heading out of the room. "I'm going to go check on him and see if he is ok. Maybe talk to our guests? Leave the water balloons out of that conversation?"

Magus smirked, "I make no promises."

Cecilia rolled her eyes and left the room to check on her father and brother.

Magus turned to look at his guests.

"Now that the nudniks are gone, let's chat."

Arianna's eyes grew huge in surprise that Magus would talk about his son and grandchildren like that. She looked at her friends, who all looked equally surprised.

"Now, now, don't look like that. There isn't much going on at the farm. It is very boring."

"Is that why you live here, sir?" Arianna ventured to ask.

Magus sighed.

"It is one of the reasons, Your Majesty. And, please, call me Magus."

"Magus, why do you live here alone?"

"Ahhhh, You Majesty, living alone is good for leaving all distractions behind. I can focus on my work as opposed to taking care of dragons all day."

"You don't like the dragons?"

"Well, I do, of course, but they require quite a lot of care and I do have things I need to study up on and focus my time on."

"Like, future telling?"

Magus scoffed. "My son makes it sound like I am a circus

freak!"

Arianna looked confused.

"What is a circus?"

"Never mind that. Tell me about your journey. I want to hear all about Eumetadotos. We left when I was a young lad. I barely remember much of it."

Arianna began to tell the stories again, Magus nodded at certain parts, making Arianna think that he had been scrying and knew about certain things. As she was talking, Améthystos's voice tinkled in her ears again, "Remember not to tell him everything, child. None of the wizards are completely safe."

Arianna finished telling the story, leaving out the same parts as she left out when she told it to Cassidy, Cecilia and Sumner.

"And what of the Stiléto me fteró drákou?"

Arianna looked surprised that he knew of the dagger.

"Yes, yes, I know of its existence. I know that it presented itself to you as well. You do not have to tell me where it is. I am sure that Améthystos has warned you not to trust us completely. However, Your Majesty, I advise you to trust us a little more than you do if we are to help you in your fight."

"Do *not* show him the dagger, child. Not until it is the right time."

"How will I know when it is the right time?" Arianna questioned Améthystos.

"You will know. Please trust me that right now is not the right time."

Arianna looked Magus in the eye.

"I do trust you. However, I must trust my dragon first and foremost. If she is telling me to keep it quiet. I must keep it quiet for now, at least."

Magus smiled brightly.

"I was hoping that you would say that. Améthystos chose well. Of course, it wasn't completely her choice, now was it? You two were fated to be bonded, weren't you?"

Arianna looked surprised again.

"Don't look so shocked, Your Highness. I told you, I am an expert on prophesies."

"He is also an expert on his ego," Améthystos's voice tinkled in Arianna's ears as she suppressed a giggle.

Magus seemed to realize that it was getting late.

"I should make you all something to eat," as he rushed from the room, leaving his guests to look at each other in amazement and confusion."

Adasser was the first to let out a chuckle.

"He sure is an odd man, isn't he?"

The rest of the group laughed out loud and stood up to follow their host.

Chapter 31

As Arianna stepped out of the front door, she took a look around the grounds. It was a beautiful scene. The grass was green in the clearing around the house. She looked over to where the dragons lay, resting and saw Améthystos and Zafeíri curled together. It looked like they were sleeping. She smiled at them and looked away.

Arianna noticed that a very large picnic table had been set up and there was already a lot of food already set out on the table. She thought it best not to ask where it all came from so quickly. She wasn't sure if she was more uneasy about the thought of Magus knowing that they were coming and started cooking earlier, or the thought of the food being conjured by magic. She went over and joined her friends.

The wizards sat at one end of the table, and Arianna and the Elves sat at the other. Arianna wound up sitting next to Sumner, who was very apparent in his displeasure as he huffed when she sat down. Arianna tried to avoid interacting with him as best as she could, not wanting to trigger his temper again.

Magus noticed the tension around the table, especially Cassidy's cold shoulder towards himself. He tried to break the ice.

"Well, I think that we should discuss whether we will go back to Eumetadotos with the queen and the elves. Don't you all?"

Sumner growled and jumped up from the table.

"SIT DOWN!" Magus's voice boomed out and reverberated all around them. Everyone froze and Sumner, slowly turned and sat back down, not taking his eyes off of Magus. There was a mixture of fear and hatred for this grandfather.

Magus went back to his normal volume, which was still loud, but not as commanding.

"Good. Now, we shall discuss going back to help."

Sumner was the first to speak. "Never. I will never go back and help them."

Magus closed his eyes and sighed deeply.

"I was afraid that you would say that, Sumner. I was hoping for a different answer from you. However, I cannot and will not coerce you into agreeing to help."

He turned his attention to Cecilia and Cassidy.

"And the two of you?"

Cecilia was squirming in her seat. "I want to go, Grandfather! Please, let me go!"

Cassidy looked uncomfortable as he shifted in his seat and said, "I will go and help."

Magus looked pleased. "You have the help of the three of

us."

He turned to Arianna and said, "Your Majesty, please ask Améthystos to alert her dragons that we are planning to help in Eumetadotos. Ask her to find any volunteers that may wish to cross back."

Arianna relayed the message to Améthystos, who answered almost immediately, "We all wish to go with you. All of us."

Arianna looked at Magus and told him, "They all wish to go."

"Splendid!"

Sumner's voice echoed around them, "Splendid? You are leading our dragons to slaughter and you think that is splendid? Grandfather, I have known you to be many things, but a cold, heartless murderer is not one of them."

With that, another water balloon fell from the sky and landed on Sumner's head. Sumner looked downright furious when it hit.

"Really? Water balloons at a time like this? Grandfather, this is not the time for childish games. We are talking about actual lives here."

Another water balloon hit and Sumner's eyes flashed in anger. His expression grew more and more ferocious and Arianna began to feel scared.

"Calm down, Sumner. Why don't you try throwing some yourself? Maybe it will get some of that rage ou –," Sumner had launched a water balloon directly at his grandfather's face, drenching him on impact.

Arianna looked around and saw buckets of water balloons all around the clearing. She looked at her friends out of the corner of her eye, silently questioning what was happening.

Cecilia jumped up and yelled, "Water balloon fight," as she launched a water balloon at Tanelia.

Arianna held her breath, waiting for the elf's response, which was to stand up, grab three and launch them back in Cecilia's direction…all three hitting their mark at once. This triggered everyone to jump up from their seats and start launching the balloons at each other, and, eventually, most of them started laughing.

Arianna looked around and realized that Magus had broken most of the tension in the group. She spotted Sumner, who actually had cracked a rare smile, and launched one in his direction. She held her breath as it broke open on his back and he turned to see who had hit him.

He walked over to her slowly and stopped right in front of her, making Arianna regret her decision to throw it at him in the first place. She was terrified of what he was going to do, until he reached up and dropped a water balloon that she didn't realize that he had been holding right onto her head, causing it to explode.

He smirked and walked away as Arianna breathed a sigh of relief.

"Don't think that this means that you've won me over, Your Majesty," he called over his shoulder. "I still have no intention of helping you."

"Well, at least he didn't kill me," Arianna thought to herself.

Améthystos's voice tinkled in her ears again, "Do not trust them completely."

Chapter 32

Magus's voice boomed through the clearing.

"Well, now that we have all gotten a little bit of tension out, why don't we retire and get some rest? We can decide on whether we shall return to Eumetadotos in the morning. You all must be very tired from your journey. I have made some rooms for you all to sleep in and I trust that they will be to your liking. Cassidy, Cecilia, Sumner, you have your usual rooms. The rest of you, follow me."

Arianna, Ellavorn, Tanelia, and Adasser followed Magus into the house, where Magus showed them each to their own rooms. Adasser and Tanelia's rooms were across from each other, as were Arianna's and Ellavorn's.

"Whatever you need, the room will provide for you. Do not hesitate to ask."

Arianna and her friends all bid each other good night and entered the rooms. Arianna looked around, and saw a bed, but nothing more. She looked confused as she sat on the bed, which felt so comfortable after spending so much time sleeping on the ground in tents. She sighed and thought,

"I sure could use a nice, hot bath."

As soon as the thought was thought in her mind, a claw-footed tub full of hot water appeared in the corner of the room. The water smelled sweet like jasmine and roses. Arianna gasped in surprise.

Améthystos's voice tinkled in her ears again.

"He did say that the room would provide for you. You are staying in a wizard's home tonight, child. It is a magical place. Whatever you want or need, just think it and it will happen."

Arianna hesitated before walking over to the tub and getting ready for her bath. She dipped in a toe and pulled it back saying, "Ohh, hot!"

Instantly, the tub stopped steaming. She looked at it again, confused and dipped her other foot in. This time, it was still hot, but comfortable. She got into the tub and laid back, her muscles all relaxing in the water. She closed her eyes and cleared her mind for the first time in weeks, looking forward to going home the next day.

After a while, she sat up and looked around for a towel, but did not find one, so she thought, "I could use a nice, warm, fluffy towel to wrap myself in to dry off."

The fluffiest towel that she had ever seen appeared next to the tub. She picked it up and wrapped it around herself, thinking how this is the softest towel she had ever used. She threw her clothes back on and she walked back to the bed and laid down, sinking into the down of the comforter that draped the bed. Before she knew it, she had fallen asleep.

Arianna's mind drifted into dream mode and she heard a voice, the voice that she feared most.

"Coming back soon, Little Queenie?"

Arianna looked around. It looked as though she was in the cellars of her castle, but one of the interior walls was reduced to a pile of rubble. She looked for the origin of the voice that so haunted her.

"You can look for me, but I will only reveal myself to you when I wish to, Queenie."

"Why are you doing this? What did we ever do to you to make you hate us so?"

The voice cackled.

"You will find out in due time, Queenie. In due time. I look forward to this fight. You do not have what it takes to defeat me. You never will. You should just stay where you are, at least you will have escaped with your life. Don't worry. I will take care of the friends you left behind. Maybe I will make their deaths painless. Perhaps not."

"Leave them alone! They didn't do anything to you!"

This seemed to anger the Dark Figure.

"You know nothing of what they have or have not done to me! You are nothing but a useless queen. Their crimes could simply be that they are associated with the likes of you."

"You will not win this fight. I will not give up that easily."

"Yes, yes, what will you do? Hurt me with your eyes? Your eyes that have been prophesized for so long? I do not fear those eyes, Queenie. I shall pluck them out when I defeat you."

Arianna made a sound of disgust.

"You are vile."

This seems to make the Dark Figure become more unhinged.

"You do not know the meaning of the word vile! Your bloodline is tainted with the most vile of them all and you speak to me of being vile. I shall snuff you out and end the disgrace that your family represents."

The Dark Figure emerged at the top of the pile of rubble, hands poised to throw a spell at Arianna, who stood ready to defend herself, when the whole room lit up with the light of flames, which encircled the entire room. Arianna and The Dark Figure both startled and turned to look at the flames, which seemed to stay in place.

Slowly, Arianna saw a path of ice start to form, inching its way over to The Dark Figure. As the ice advanced, the fire followed. Arianna watched in amazement as the ice led the fire to the bottom or the rubble heap. The Dark Figure saw what was happening and shrieked in anger as it realized that the fire was making its way towards it.

"You will pay, Queenie. Along with your dragon as well."

There was a crack and some smoke, and The Dark Figure disappeared from the top of the rubble where it stood just a moment before. The flames extinguished after a few seconds. Arianna sat straight up in bed, wide awake now, and looked around in disbelief.

"Améthystos, was that you that helped me just now?"

"Yes, child. Are you ok?"

"I – I think so. That was just a dream, right?"

"Dreams are just reality while sleeping. Yes, that was a dream, however, that attack was real. Exercise caution, child. This thing is more dangerous than I imagined."

"Améthystos?"

"Yes, child?"

"Thank you for helping me just now."

The tinkling laugh echoed in her ears again.

"You are welcome, child. We cannot die before the battle has even begun, can we?"

"No, we cannot. I do not intend on dying any time soon."

"Now, that is the attitude I like to hear from you."

"Améthystos?"

"Yes, child?"

"Do you think we have a chance to win this battle?"

"I think that you are the best chance that we all have of surviving."

"I will try my best to defeat this thing."

"I know you will, child. Now, rest. I will keep guard over you tonight."

Arianna sank back into the bed and fell back to sleep, this time, no more dreams awaited her and she slept soundly until morning light.

Chapter 33

Arianna's eyes flickered open as the light started to shine into her room. She stretched and walked to the window, and saw the dragons all relaxing together in the field. She was taking in the scenery when she noticed Cassidy and Sumner having a heated discussion. She couldn't hear what they were saying, but she could guess that Sumner was not happy about what was being discussed.

After a short moment, he threw his hands up in disgust and stormed away from his father while Cassidy took two futile steps towards his son before he realized that it was no use to chase him. He brought his hand to his forehead and started to rub his temples, as if trying to massage out a migraine.

Arianna watched him for a moment, when Cassidy raised his head and looked up at her window and saw her standing there. She gave him a small smile and waved. He returned the wave, but not the smile.

"Well, it's a start, I guess," she thought.

Just then, there was a knock at her door. She turned and went to open it. On the other side stood Adasser, Tanelia, and Ellavorn. None of them looked as though they had slept well.

"Is everything ok with the three of you? You look exhausted."

They looked at each other in surprise.

"Didn't you hear it all night?" Adasser asked.

"Hear what? I didn't hear anything."

"Arianna, that thing was cackling all night long. It found us here somehow. I don't know how, but it did," Tanelia said.

"I didn't hear it cackling all night, but it did try to attack me in my dream last night."

"Correction, child, it *did* attack you in your dream last night."

Arianna rolled her eyes and said, "I'm sorry, I am being corrected. It did attack me in my dream last night."

The others looked around in confusion. Arianna thought, "I could really use some chairs right now for my guests."

With that, three chairs appeared for each of the elves to sit on. They all looked confused.

"Where did those chairs come from? They weren't here a moment ago."

They then looked around the room and noticed the bathtub.

"Why did you get a bathtub? None of us did."

Arianna giggled and said, "I asked the room for the bathtub

last night and the chairs just now."

They all looked at her in confusion.

"Magus told us that if we needed anything, all we had to do is ask."

Ellavorn said, "We thought he meant him, not the room!"

With that, a large glass of water appeared in his hands.

"Well, would you look at that? It worked!"

"Focus, Ellavorn," Tanelia scolded him.

"Arianna, tell us about the attack. What happened? Did it give you any more of a clue as to who or what it is?"

"No, I didn't see anything indicating who it could be. I was in one of the cellars, but it was damaged. The all had be knocked down, and it was a big pile of rubble. The Dark Figure started to laugh, but it was hiding at first. It appeared on top of the rubble and was ready to attack. I was ready to defend myself, but then the perimeter of the entire room went up in flames. They were odd flames, though. There was ice around the base and it seemed to lead the flames to where it wanted them to go. The ice was moving towards the Dark Figure, but I guess it realized it was coming for it and disappeared."

"Where did the flames come from?" Ellavorn was curious to know.

"Améthystos. She protected me. She has both ice and fire powers, remember?"

Tanelia shifted in her seat and tried to hide it when she rubbed her bottom, where she had fallen when Améthystos turned the ground beneath her to ice. Arianna bit her bottom lip to keep from laughing out loud, which drew a fierce look from Tanelia, which made Arianna forget about laughing.

"We need to get back to Eumetadotos quickly," Adasser said.

Arianna looked uneasy. "We have to find out if the wizards are going to help us first. We need their help in this battle."

Arianna felt a tingling sensation in her fingers. She wiggled them around to get rid of it, causing the others to look at her strangely.

"I just felt like I had pins and needles in my fingers."

"Wait, Arianna, you just said that we need the wizards help," Ellavorn said. With that, he started waving his fingers around.

"I just got the same sensation in my fingers. Do you think that the room is doing something because we said we needed it?"

Arianna looked as though she had had an epiphany. "Adasser, Tanelia, you say it too."

Both looked uncomfortable.

"Arianna, we cannot do that," Adasser said.

"Why not? We do need their help."

Adasser and Tanelia both shook their heads and looked at Ellavorn.

"Arianna, we have to take it back. If this room is required to give us what we ask for, we cannot ask for this. It would take away the wizards' free will and that goes against our code."

Arianna looked disappointed, but agreed that it wouldn't be fair to influence their decision in this matter.

"I take it back. I need the wizards to make their decision on whether to help on their own."

Ellavorn said the same thing and the tingling in their fingers stopped.

Arianna looked at her friends and said, "I guess we will have to leave this up to trust."

They all nodded in agreement and got up to leave. Arianna was the last to exit. Before she did, she turned and took one last look around and whispered, "Thank you for everything."

The room seemed to sparkle a bit, but she just credited that to her imagination, knowing that the room is magic.

She turned and walked out the door, catching up to her friends on their way to meet up with the wizards to hear what decision had been made in regards to their return.

Chapter 34

Arianna and the elves wandered outside and found the wizards, except for Sumner, sitting around the table from last night, talking. Cassidy noticed them approaching first and nodded to Arianna and motioned for them to sit down. The four of them took their seats and said their good mornings.

"How did you sleep last night," Magus asked.

Arianna looked at him and said, "The bed was very comfortable, but I was visited by the Dark Figure last night."

The wizards all snapped to attention at this information.

Cassidy spoke first, "What do you mean, you were attacked? What happened?"

Arianna filled them in on what had happened the night before. When she looked back up, she noticed that all of their faces had grown pale.

"Améthystos used the fire and ice at the same time?" Cassidy inquired.

Arianna nodded, "Yee, she saved me from the battle with The Dark Figure."

Cassidy rubbed the bridge of his nose with his thumb and forefinger and then looked at his father.

"You know what this means, don't you father?"

"It means that we have no choice in the matter anymore, Cassidy. We must *all* go back to Eumetadotos."

Cassidy sighed. "Sumner is not going to like this."

Cecilia piped up, "Sumner will have to get over it. We need him to be on board with us. He is very powerful, Father, we all know this. He will have to help us."

Arianna was looking from one of the wizards to the other, waiting for a lull in the conversation.

"I am confused. What does this all mean?"

Magus looked over at her as if he had forgotten that she was there.

"Your Majesty, this means that we must return with you or our bloodline will be in danger next. You see, if a creature that powerful can find in in both realms, it can decide to attack us as well."

Cassidy began to run his temples. Arianna could send his stress level growing by the moment. She could tell that he was conflicted as to what to do next.

"Arianna, you have our allegiance," Cassidy said hesitantly.

"Cassidy, I only want you to come back if you want to come back. I don't want you to feel obligated to help if you do not want to."

Cassidy sighed, "Please, do not think that I do not wish to help. I truly do. I just...I don't know how much help I, in particular, can be."

"How do you mean?" Arianna inquired, feigning ignorance.

Cassidy bowed his head. "Arianna, I cannot use magic. I am bound. I do not know how much help I can be."

Arianna looked him in the eye and told him, "I have others on my side who have no magic and no powers. There is always a way to help, Cassidy. I do mean it when I say that if you do not feel comfortable helping, you do not have to come back."

"No, I pledged my allegiance, and I am loyal to my word."

Arianna smiled and nodded.

"Ok, we need to figure out how to get everyone back to Eumetadotos. I know of the dragon scales, however, Améthystos has said that the dragons left back at your place wish to join the fight. How shall we get them back?"

Cassidy and Magus looked at each other.

"I will take Sumner with me and round them up. Cassidy,

you and Cecilia go on with our friends. We will meet you there. I may be able to talk some sense into the boy as well."

Cassidy and Cecilia nodded in understanding.

"Ok, let's eat our breakfast and get everything ready for our tip back."

As Magus announced that, food appeared on the table, ready to eat. Cassidy went in and summoned Sumner back outside, where he reluctantly sat down to eat, his sneer demonstrating just how deep his dislike for Arianna and the elves resided inside of him. There was no mistake the absolute disdain he held for Eumetadotos and it made Arianna doubt that Magus could change his mind on the matter. The meal was uncomfortably quiet.

When breakfast had finished, they all dispersed to get their things ready for the trip back.

Adasser grabbed Arianna by the arm.

"Arianna, do you trust them?

"Adasser, we have no choice but to trust them. We need their help. They are coming back with us to help. We cannot risk doing anything that will cause them to back out. I know that there are things they may be holding back, but we are too."

Adasser nodded.

"Cassidy being bound worries me. Unbound wizards can

become unstable, unpredictable. Why is he making the journey back with us instead of Magus? We came to find Magus. That was the point of coming here."

"We did find Magus. We need him to convince Sumner to come back and help too. He seems to be able to reach the twins on a deeper level than Cassidy can. I think he may be hoping to take advantage of that and get Sumner to return."

Adasser nodded again.

"I will keep a watchful eye on Cassidy."

Arianna nodded back at him and smiled.

"I think that we will be safe with him."

"Are you looking forward to returning home?"

Arianna smiled again.

"I am. I am eager to see Abigail again. Poor Joshua has been asleep since before we left. We need to wake him up. We also have the dilemma of Iron Demon."

"Yes, the pirate. That issue should be dealt with quickly."

"Yes, that should probably be the first task."

Tanelia slowly walked over to them, looking as though she had just thought of something of the utmost importance.

"Arianna?"

"Yes, Tanelia?"

"We're riding the dragons back, correct?"

"Yes."

"Uhhhh, what are they going to think when we appear through a portal riding a bunch of dragons?"

Arianna's eyes grew huge.

"I didn't even think of that. I know how we felt when we wandered up on them all grazing. The sight of dragons walking back into our realm, well, it would be rather shocking."

"That's why I'm asking you about this."

"I think that we should probably ask Magus about how to go about going back in the safest manner."

"Yeah, that would probably be a good idea. I know that the elves would open fire on any dragon that they may see. It is in our training."

Arianna nodded and found Magus to ask about the situation.

"Well, now, I never thought about that."

He glanced at the dragons, who seemed to be getting antsy

in anticipation of their journey home.

"That is a lot of dragon blood to be spilled if they are attacked. Where would be a safe place for them to cross over?"

Arianna thought about it for a moment, not quite sure as to an exact safe location.

"I wish that I could communicate with them to let them know that we are coming back and bringing dragons with us."

"There is a way, child." Améthystos's voice tinkled in her ears again.

"How?"

"Come see me."

"Améthystos said there is a way to communicate with them. I have to go see her."

"I am coming with you. These dragons. They never cease to amaze me."

They reached where Améthystos lay and she pulled a scale from her body and laid it at Arianna's feet.

"Press the scale with your thumb and think of who you wish to speak with."

Arianna picked up the scale and tried to think of who she should contact first. The only person on her mind was Abigail. She realized just how much she missed her dear friend. So, she closed her eyes and pictured her face in her mind and rubbed the scale.

"Arianna? Is that you?"

Arianna opened her eyes and saw a small portal opened before her.

"Abigail! I have missed you! I don't have much time, but I need to tell you that we are coming home today. But, we are bringing some...guests."

"You found him? You found Magus?"

Arianna nodded and laughed. "Yes, we found Magus, his son, Cassidy and his twins, Cecilia and Sumner. Cassidy and Cecilia are coming back with us now. Magus and Sumner will join us later."

"Why aren't they all coming together?"

"Well, that is why I am contacting you. You see, we're sort of bringing some dragons back too."

"DRAGONS? DID YOU SAY DRAGONS? Oh, no, Ari, this is bad. This is very, very bad."

"No, Abigail, there is no time to explain. My time is almost up. Please, tell the others that I command that no dragon will harmed when we come back. Not a scale!"

"I will let them know."

The portal was starting to close as the scale was losing some of its power and it continued to shrink.

"I have to go. We will be back today, as soon as we are finished here. Remember, Abigail, not a single scale!"

"You have my word, Ari!"

The portal closed as Abigail said those last words.

"Can you trust your friend to get the message back? As much as the dragons are burdensome, I do not wish for them to be injured."

Arianna looked at Magus and smiled.

"Oh, Abigail is the person I trust most over there. She will get the word out. Do not fret."

Magus nodded, relief in his eyes.

"Each of the dragons will need to open their own portal. The scales would not have enough magic to keep the portals open for all of them to pass through."

"Noted."

Just then, Adasser, Ellavorn, Tanelia, Cecilia and Cassidy came walking over.

Cassidy looked at the dragons and back at the traveling party.

"We are ready to do this."

Arianna noticed that he and Cecilia were a little apprehensive.

"Are the two of you ok with this?"

They both nodded in agreement.

Cecilia spoke first, "I am nervous. I have always wanted to see Eumetadotos, and now, I am getting my wish."

Arianna smiled. "I wish that it was under better circumstances."

Cassidy shifted from foot to foot as they spoke.

"I just hope that I will be able to help in some way. I feel helpless."

Arianna walked over to him and put her hand on his shoulder.

"I did not lie to you when I told you that we have non-magical people helping us. We can get you some training on how to defend yourself without magic."

Cassidy gave a weak smile.

Magus's voice boomed out again.

"Ok, everyone, mount your dragons. They will all select a scale for you. Hold that scale in your hands, and think of the castle in Eumetadotos. A portal will open for you to go through. Once you cross over, let go of the scales to close it behind you. Sumner and I will join you in a few days' time with the rest of the dragons. Good luck."

The travelers all climbed up onto their dragons. The dragons all plucked a scale for each one and laid them in their hands. The next thing Arianna knew, six portals had opened up, all of them had a clear vision of the castle on the other side. She could hear Cecilia's breath catch and she smiled.

"Let's roll," she heard Cassidy yell out and each of the dragons walked through their respective portals.

They all dropped the scales as soon as they were on the other side, leaving the portals to close behind them. Only one word thundered in Arianna's mind as she slid down from Améthystos.

"Home!"

Chapter 35

"ARI, YOU'RE BACK!!!" Arianna didn't have a chance to brace herself when Abigail slammed into her, knocking her back a few steps, making her laugh as she hugged her best friend back. After a moment, Abigail turned to look around at the newcomers and sucked in her breath at the sight of the dragons, her face turning pale.

"Ari, you weren't kidding when you said you were bringing back dragons!"

"Abigail, please tell me that you alerted everyone not to harm them?!?!"

Abigail nodded. "Yes, I let them all know not to harm a single scale."

"We would like to know why you have brought dragons back to Eumetadotos, though," Armen's voice called out.

Ellavorn watched as his father calmly walked over and embraced him.

"I have missed you, my son."

He turned back to Arianna.

"Now, can you please explain how they exist at all and why have you brought them here? Dragons are dangerous creatures."

Arianna smiled.

"These dragons are not dangerous, Armen. You can tell by their scales."

Armen seemed to just notice the beautiful jewel-toned scales on the dragons and looked at Arianna curiously.

"Go on."

"You see, when a dragon has good in their heart, the scales will stay the jewel-tone color that they are born with. It is only when they choose evil that their color turns. As you can see, all of our dragons still have their jewel tones."

"*Your* dragons?"

Arianna stammered, "Well, you see, ummm, yes. These dragons have pledged themselves to us. Ellavorn and Zafeíri. Adasser and Tourkouáz. Tanelia and Akouamarínis. We must protect them at all costs. Their lives are bound to ours now. If something happens to us, they will die."

Armen had a look of fear spread across his face.

"And if they die first? Will you die as well?"

"No. It is the risk that the dragon takes when bonding themselves to someone."

She looked at Améthystos and smiled, "I think that this is

the deepest expression of trust, don't you?"

Arianna swore it looked like Améthystos smiled. She looked back to Armen.

"As long as they are bonded to someone and that someone stays on the path of good, we will be safe."

Armen nodded.

Cassidy cleared his throat.

Arianna jumped and exclaimed, "I am sorry, I have forgotten my manners. Armen, this is Cassidy and his daughter, Cecilia. They are the heirs to the wizard."

"I thought you were going to find Magus?"

"We did. He and Sumner, Cecilia's twin, were going back to get the other dragons. They should be joining us in the next few days with more."

"*More*? How many more?"

Cassidy spoke this time, "There are ten left at the farm, in addition to the ones that Sumner and my father are riding."

"A dozen more dragons? Coming here?"

"Yes, sir."

"How can we guarantee that they will not turn on us? We

cannot have any more danger in these parts. An evil dragon could demolish this kingdom in no time flat."

"We are aware of the ramifications of a turned dragon," Cassidy said, his voice laced with venom. "We will take precautions to keep that from happening."

"And just what *precautions* are you going to take?"

Cecilia stepped in front of her father, the disdain she felt towards Armen was flowing off of her in waves.

"As my father as said, we will do what we feel necessary to keep that from happening. Our dragons do not have evil in their hearts. They are not bred to hate. They are only bred with love and peace. We will not have an issue."

Armen looked Cecilia up and down, assessing her attitude towards him. He raised his eyebrows and said, "Very well. Where are they going to stay? Surely you cannot fir one dragon in the castle, let alone six now and a dozen more later."

Arianna hadn't thought about that.

"Don't worry, child, we will protect the perimeter of the castle in shifts," Améthystos voice tinkled in her ears again. Arianna had started to love the sound of her voice. It made her feel calm and safe.

"The dragons will patrol the outside of the castle in shifts, I am told. Armen, I trust that you have spread the word to The Forest Glen that not one scale shall be harmed on these dragons, am I correct?"

"Yes, your majesty."

"ARIANNA!!!!!!"

Charlie came running out of the castle, and then stopped dead in his tracks when he saw the dragons. His face wore a mixture of fear and delight at the sight of the dragons.

"DRAGONS!!!!"

Arianna laughed, and he started running full force towards her again. She threw her arms out and caught him, twirling him in the air. She placed him back on his feet and patted his head.

"I swear, you've grown a so much since I last saw you, Charlie!"

Charlie beamed with pride. "I am quite bigger now."

Arianna laughed and turned back to Armen.

"I believe we have some things to discuss now that we are all here."

Armen nodded, "Let us talk in the Odigós Domátio."

"The Odigós Domátio? I have only heard tales of it from my grandfather. I would like to see it myself. Is this permissible?"

Armen looked at Cassidy and nodded, then make a gesture to follow him.

Arianna looked to Améthystos and smiled.

"Welcome home."

"Thank you, child."

They all turned and started walking into the castle and down to the Odigós Domátio to discuss what had happened and strategy going forward."

Chapter 36

The group arrived in the kitchen and Armen placed the key into the slot and the steps opened up for them all to enter the Odigós Domátio. The elves, Abigail and Charlie all started the descent. Cassidy and Cecilia stood, frozen in place, staring down at the steps in reverence.

"Cassidy, Cecilia, are you ok?"

Cassidy looked at her, tears filling his eyes.

"I have only heard of the Odigós Domátio in tales from when I was a little boy, and them my father re-telling the stories again to my children. It is like a fairy tale that has come to life."

Arianna smiled.

"It is pretty remarkable. Do you need a moment before you enter?"

"No, I am ready." He turned to Cecilia and asked, "Are you ready to see the famous room of your ancestors?"

Cecilia smiled broadly and nodded excitedly.

Arianna led the way down. She could hear Cassidy and Cecilia's excited gasps when their feet touched the bottom of the stairs. Both of their faces were filled with awe as they took in everything around them.

"May we look around?" Cecilia was beside herself with excitement.

"Of course. Would you like me to go with you?"

Cecilia nodded. With that, Charlie was by Arianna's side again.

"Arianna, may I go with you? I got real good at doing magic!" He turned to Cecilia.

"I can read ALLLLLLLLLLLLLL of these books!"

Cecilia laughed. "Are you a wizard too?"

Charlie stood as tall as he could make himself, puffed his little chest out in pride and nodded. Cecilia laughed again.

"Well, you will have to show us what you have learned. You know, I'm a wizard too."

"Are you one of the people Arianna was looking for?"

"Well, she came to my realm looking for my grandfather, Magus. We all decided to come back and help too."

"Can you teach me stuff?"

Cecilia gave him a thoughtful look.

"I can, but I am better at alchemy than I am at spellcasting. My twin brother, Sumner, is better at spell casting."

Charlie looked around, confused.

"Where is he at? Will he teach me stuff?"

Cecilia looked a bit unsure.

"Well, little guy, I can't make any promises on my brother's behalf. He is quite…difficult."

"Why?"

"Well, he doesn't quite like Eumetadotos. I think he holds a grudge from when our great-grandfather was banished from here."

"Oh. Do you not like us too?"

"I like you just fine. I'm not too sure about the elves, though. I don't trust them."

"But, the elves have been helping us. They are good. They like us."

Cecilia smiled.

"I'm sure they have been good to you. Now, are you going to give me a tour or what?"

"Yes! Let's go," Charlie exclaimed and started running off with Cecilia laughing and trying to keep up.

Arianna called over, "I'm going to go fill Armen in on what is happening."

She got no response back, but could hear Cecilia and Charlie giggling so she smiled and walked over to Armen and the others.

"Where are Cassidy and Cecilia?"

"They wanted to take a look around the Odigós Domátio. It has been a century since someone from their bloodline has stepped foot in this room. Give them a few minutes."

Armen nodded. "That is fine. In the meantime, please fill us in on your journey."

Arianna, Adasser, Ellavorn and Tanelia all began to take turns telling the story of how they had four dragons bond themselves to them and the journey to find Magus. They were finishing the story when Cassidy, Cecilia and Charlie came back. Charlie had his hands full of books. Armen looked at the books and sighed.

"Young Charlie has been devouring those books since you left. It is all he can think about. He has gotten quite good at spell—"a crash and a bright light flashed in the corner of the room.

Armen closed his eyes in frustration, chanting under his breath, "He is just a child. He is just a child."

Arianna deduced that this was a common occurrence since Charlie called from that side of the room, "Oops. It's ok! I got it!"

She looked from the direction of the corner, to Armen and back again.

"Would you care to explain that?"

Armen sighed.

"Young Charlie has become obsessed with learning the fireball spell. It is the first one that he has not been able to master right away."

Another crash and bright light.

"He has been…practicing."

Arianna bit her lip to keep from laughing. Armen looked very stressed out over this spell, and from the level of exasperation she saw on his face, she could tell that Charlie was determined to practice until he got the spell perfect.

Another crash and bright light, this time, it was followed by a yelp from Cassidy.

"OK, Charlie, how about you practice some more later? We have to get Cassidy and Cecilia in here to talk strategy."

Charlie, Cecilia and Cassidy came back into the main section of the room. Cassidy was rubbing his hand with an annoyed look on his face.

"Awwww, ok! But, I'm really starting to get good!"

Cassidy spoke up, "When my father gets here, he may have some tips for you, kid."

"Really? Wow! Thank you! But, wait, how come *you* can't show me anything?"

The room went silent, with all eyes on Cassidy. Arianna didn't know whether to say anything or not. She didn't want to tell Cassidy's secret and betray his trust. Cassidy looked around the room, then looked back at Charlie, swallowed and said, "Well, because I am unable to do magic. I am bound."

Armen gasped. Abigail and Charlie looked confused.

"What does that mean, bound?" Abigail asked first.

"It means that I am no longer able to do magic. I have had the ability taken away."

"But – why?"

"It is a story for another time. I have come here, willing to do what I can to help in this fight. I will do just that."

Armen spoke up. "We needed the Wizard's magic."

"And you shall have that with my daughter, my father, and my son, should he choose to join us."

"He has not made the decision to join us?"

"No. He has not."

"Father, Grandfather will do everything he can to get him to join us in this fight."

Cassidy looked at Cecilia.

"Cecilia, there are some things that even the Mighty Magus cannot do. Unfortunately, I believe that this is one of them. If Sumner chooses not to join us, then we will figure this fight out without him."

Cecilia looked crestfallen at the idea that her brother may not join.

"In terms of strategy, I believe that we should wait for my father to join us. He has some expertise in strategy. I, however, do not. He would be the best one to ask."

Armen agreed.

"Abigail, Charlie, why don't you show our new friends to their chambers? I am sure that they must be exhausted from the day's journey."

They nodded and Charlie started racing up the stairs.

"Abigail, meet me in my chambers later?"

Abigail smiled, nodded and started up the stairs after Cassidy, Cecilia and Charlie.

Arianna turned to Armen.

"Now, we need to wake up Iron Demon and coerce him into abdicating back to me."

Armen nodded and led the way.

Chapter 37

Arianna, Armen, Adasser, Ellavorn and Tanelia began their descent into the dungeons where Iron Demon was being kept.

"Armen, do you have the Elixir with you?"

"Of course I do, Arianna. I have been coming down here faithfully every day to give him just enough to keep him alive. I dare not wake him from his deep sleep. I was waiting for you to return before awakening him so that we can restore your rightful place in Eumetadotos."

Arianna nodded in approval.

They arrived at Iron Demon's cell and Adasser went in first, tying him down to the bed so that Iron Demon could not escape when they gave him the elixir. They formed a semi-circle around him and Armen gave him a full dose to wake him up.

"Where am I?" Iron Demon screeched as he woke up and noticed that he was in a dungeon surrounded by the Elves and Arianna.

He sneered at Arianna.

"You tricked me! You cursed me!"

Arianna shook her head.

"No, it wasn't I who cursed you. The Dark Figure cursed

the titles of King and Queen."

"You knew when you abdicated to me that this would happen," his sneer was getting deeper.

Arianna nodded.

"I did."

"You bitch. You let me take your title, knowing that it would cause me pain!"

"I let you take the title, knowing that it would cause you *death*."

"And they say that I am vile? You tricked me!"

Ellavorn stepped forward.

"You have been involved with more trickery than any living creature alive."

"Silence from you, *traitor*."

"I will not stay silent while you insult and threaten my fiancée."

Several surprised gasps were heard.

"Oh, so you're planning on marrying this bitch again?"

"I am planning on marrying Arianna, the rightful queen of Eumetadotos."

Iron Demon began to laugh maniacally.

"You want to take on this pain for yourself?"

Arianna stepped forward.

"I am going to take that pain back. Armen gave you enough of the elixir to wake you up for a short while with no pain. It should be wearing off soon. If you abdicate back to me, you will not endure any more pain."

"I will still be stuck in this dungeon."

"Are you saying that you wish to make a deal?"

Iron Demon looked defeated. He was bound to the bed in his cell with no other option. He sighed

"I will make a deal," he spat out.

"You must abdicate the title back to me, and we will set you free. Should you try to attack any one of use, Adasser and Tanelia will kill you in an instant."

Iron Demon chuckled.

"You think that either of them would be able to overpower me? I am the most feared pirate in the realm."

"And they are the two top ranked Defenders of the Forest Glen. Do you want to take your chances?"

Iron Demon looked between Tanelia and Adasser, both of whom had their hands on their weapons, ready to strike. He laughed at the sight.

"Fine, I will abdicate to you, no trickery involved."

Ellavorn spoke up, "Do we have your word?"

Iron Demon sighed, "You have my word and my word is my bond."

Ellavorn nodded and Arianna stepped forward and took hold of Iron Demon's hand.

"You still have soft hands, Your Majesty."

"Stop talking to me, you vile being."

Armen performed the ceremony again and there was a swirling of the wind as the title transferred back from Iron Demon to Arianna. Followed by a black mist that emerged slowly from Iron Demon's stomach and plunged itself into Arianna's stomach. She screamed in pain. Armen quickly gave her the Elixir and the pain subsided.

"Ellavorn, take Arianna up to her chambers. Adasser, Tanelia, make sure that Iron Demon gets out of the kingdom immediately."

Both nodded and each grabbed one of Iron Demon's arms. Armen freed him and they tied his hands behind him and led him to the castle.

"We shall take him to the other edge of the woods and let him loose. We shall return after we free him."

"Very well. Be safe, my friends."

Adasser and Tanelia turned and pushed Iron Demon to get him to move. He started moving in the direction of the stables. Adasser and Tanelia looked at each other and smiled. The ground started to shake as Tourkouáz and Akouamarínis came bounding over, skidding to a stop in front of them.

They snuck a look at Iron Demon's face, from which all of the blood had drained as his brain registered what was going on.

"D-d-d-dragons?"

Adasser pushed him towards Tourkouáz.

"Yes, dragons."

"That is impossible. Dragons are extinct."

"Not anymore. You're riding on one."

Adasser pushed Iron Demon up and then he mounted Tourkouáz right behind him. Both dragons flapped their wings and prepared to take off.

"Just so you know, you're going to hate this. Oh, and don't think about doing anything stupid. The dragons can, and will finish you off if you do."

With that, the dragons took off at full speed, as Iron Demon let out a scream.

Adasser spoke directly to Tourkouáz, "Good job, Dragon."

Tourkouáz's laugh sounded in Adasser's ears. "Can I make him scream again, sir? That was ever so much fun!"

Adasser fought to keep a smile from spreading across his face.

"Just once more."

Tourkouáz pulled in his wings and let himself free fall. As they were plummeting back down to the ground, Iron Demon screamed again.

Tourkouáz flapped his wings and they were air born again. He did a barrel roll while laughing. Iron Demon passed out.

"Well, at least I won't have to deal with him screaming anymore," Adasser said.

Chapter 38

Ellavorn and Arianna started making their way to Arianna's chambers, his arm around her waist to support her while she walked.

"I forgot how much this curse makes me so tired."

Ellavorn looked at her with concern.

"I can try to cure it. I don't know if I can, but I can try."

Arianna smiled up at him.

"That would be lovely. But, first, we need to wake Joshua up."

Ellavorn groaned softly.

"Ellavorn! You promised! We need his help in this fight."

"I know. I know. I will wake him up. I just am worried that he will try to get in your way of fulfilling your destiny."

Arianna nodded.

"Yes, he has…reservations…about my powers. I have tried to talk to him about it. I think that the tendency to protect the Royal Family is ingrained so deeply in him. It scared him that I started to be able to defend myself."

"He needs to accept that you have a destiny to fulfill and

that involves being in harm's way. I don't like that idea myself, but I know that you are capable of succeeding. I am proud of you."

Arianna stopped and turned to face Ellavorn.

"Thank you. You don't know how much that means to me to know that you will be by my side."

Ellavorn held her hand in his. He lifted it to his mouth and kissed her knuckles lightly.

"It is my pleasure."

Arianna smiled and they continued walking to her room.

"I will tell you, Arianna, if he tries to get in your way, I will have to…intervene."

"What does that mean?" Arianna asked as they arrived at her bedroom door.

Ellavorn smiled and opened the door for her, and as she stepped in, Abigail jumped on her again in excitement.

"I am so glad that you are back! I want to hear all about your journey. Tell me everything…especially about the dragons! Ari, *dragons*! DRAGONS!"

Arianna giggled at her friend's enthusiasm and realized just how much she missed her as well.

"Abigail, I want to tell you all about it, but first, we have to go wake Joshua up from his sleep."

Abigail drew in a sharp breath, making piquing Arianna's curiosity.

"Is everything ok?"

"Oh, yes, of course. I just didn't realize that you knew how to wake him up."

"Well, I don't, but Ellavorn can. It is within his realm of capabilities."

Abigail looked over at Ellavorn, as if noticing for the first time that he was there.

"You are going to wake him up?"

Ellavorn nodded. "Yes, I made a promise to Arianna and I intend to keep that promise."

Abigail looked him up and down, as if assessing his honesty and nodded.

"You aren't going to try to harm him, are you?"

Ellavorn's brow knitted in confusion.

"Why should I harm the Captain?"

Abigail smirked.

"Well, he was engaged to Arianna after you left. I just

thought that the jealousy might get the better of you."

"Abigail!" Arianna hissed.

Ellavorn smiled.

"I assure you, Miss Abigail, I am not jealous of Captain Oakford."

Abigail rolled her eyes at his assurance, forcing Ellavorn to try even harder not to laugh.

"Abigail, what has gotten into you?"

"Ari, I have been here with Joshua while you were gone. I have kept a watchful eye on him the entire time that you were all gallivanting with wizards and dragons and whatever else you were doing. I don't know what Prince Ellavorn's intentions are with him, but I feel as though I should protect him."

"Abigail, if you do not believe him, let me assure you that Ellavorn will not harm Joshua. I'm more afraid of Joshua trying to harm him."

Ellavorn jolted and looked at her.

"Whatever do you mean, you are afraid he will try to hurt me?"

Arianna shifted from one foot to the other.

"Well, you know that Joshua is a little…overprotective."

"Yes."

"I'm not sure how he will take the news."

Abigail's ears perked up.

"News? What news?"

Arianna looked at her best friend then back at Ellavorn. Without saying a word, we walked over to her dresser and took out her engagement ring and slipped it on her finger again.

"Ellavorn and I are betrothed again."

Abigail threw her head back and groaned.

"Again?"

Arianna laughed.

"Yes. This is how it should have been all along, Abigail. You know that my love for Ellavorn has always been unwavering."

"What about Joshua? I thought you loved him too?"

Ellavorn let out a small groan as Arianna sighed.

"Abigail, I love Joshua in a completely different way. I never felt for him what I feel for Ellavorn. You know this. If it weren't for the curse, I would never have agreed to marry him in the first place. Yes, I love him, but in the same way that I love you."

Abigail looked disappointed in this revelation.

"I know that you never really felt that way for Joshua. I guess I just always hoped that your affection for him would grow into something more."

"I think I did too, but with Ellavorn's return, I know that it is not an option. We should go and wake him up. He has been asleep for far too long."

"Ari, what shall we do with him when he wakes up?"

"What do you mean?"

"He has been asleep for weeks. He will be in no position to fight in this battle. He will need to be kept safe."

Ellavorn cleared his throat.

"When I revive him, I will make sure that his strength is restored as well. We will need his strength and his courage to help in this fight, Miss Abigail. Just as we will need your help as well."

Abigail looked at Ellavorn with distrust in her eyes yet again.

"You left and joined with Iron Demon. You betrayed her and now she is taking you back again. Just because Ari trusts you doesn't mean that I automatically have to as well."

"Abigail! I will explain everything once we awaken Joshua.

You will understand more after that. Please be civil to Ellavorn. He honestly has everyone's best intentions at heart."

Abigail rolled her eyes and, in a huff, stormed out of the room, turning in the direction of Joshua's room.

Arianna bit her lip to keep herself from bursting into laughter at her friend's hissy fit.

"I think she means for us to follow her," Arianna said.

Ellavorn held his arm out to her and she looped hers into his and they left the room, following after Abigail.

Chapter 39

When Arianna and Ellavorn reached Joshua's door, it was left ajar and Abigail was sitting in a chair next to the head of his bed. She was speaking softly to him, unaware that she wasn't alone.

"Joshua, Arianna is back. She and Ellavorn are on their way now to awaken you from this sleep."

Joshua lay still on the bed, not giving any indication that he had heard Abigail's words, however, he could hear every one of them, although, he still couldn't place her voice. He hated being stuck in this state. He felt useless and vulnerable. He also was not happy to hear that Arianna had the elf with her again. He could only imagine what that could mean, and he did not like where his imagination took him.

The next thing he knew, he felt hands on his chest and could hear soft words being spoken. A bright light started to form and he felt a warmth unlike any other he had ever felt. The slight swirled around and around. It was breathtakingly beautiful and he was mesmerized by it. The warmth given off by the light started to spread through and absorb into his body as his muscles seemed to come to life again and he regained control of his body.

Joshua's eyes started to move and his eyelids flickered as he opened them. He winced from the sunlight streaming into his window and he gasped.

Arianna and Abigail both stood next to his bed, watching everything that happened. Their eyes flickering from Ellavorn to Joshua and back.

Joshua allowed his eyes to adjust to the light, as he felt his strength creeping back into his body. He looked around at his visitors, his eyes falling on Abigail and Arianna, then noticing Ellavorn on the other side of the bed, his hand still on Joshua's chest, as he sat with his eyes closed, and quietly muttering words over him.

Joshua sat up and slapped Ellavorn's hand away, yelling,

"Do not touch me!"

"Joshua!" Arianna scolded.

He looked at her with a look of contempt.

"Ellavorn was healing you. Without him, you would still be in that cursed slumber. Let him finish so that you can get your strength back."

"No need, Arianna, he pushed my hand away as I finished. He should have his full strength back."

Joshua growled at him, "Should we test that theory?" He made to get up from the bed.

"I would not advise trying something that stupid, Captain Oakford," Ellavorn said calmly.

"Or what?"

As Joshua finished that word, one of Tanelia's knives flew across the room and embedded itself in the wall. Everyone in the room froze.

"Or you will have to deal with me," Tanelia said as she stepped into the room and retrieved her knife.

"Do I make myself clear, *Captain?*"

Joshua sighed and muttered something about elves.

"I asked you a question, Captain Oakford. I expect an answer."

Joshua looked at her with a rage in his eyes.

"You have made yourself perfectly clear."

"Good." Tanelia turned to Arianna.

"You should be resting. Your body is not used to the Argós Thánatos anymore. Now that it is back, you need to readjust. Go back to your chambers and rest."

Arianna put her hand on Tanelia's arm.

"I am fine, Tanelia. I promise. We needed to wake Joshua

from his sleep. I will rest momentarily. I need to fill Abigail and Joshua in on what has happened. That is, if Joshua is still willing to help us in this fight?"

All eyes turned to Joshua, who was sitting up in his bed, stewing silently. He looked at each and every face in the crowd before sighing a sigh of defeat.

"Eumetadotos is my home and I have sworn to protect it. Of course I will not abandon that promise. You have my word."

Arianna smiled widely at him.

"Thank you, Joshua."

He shook his head, and finally noticed the ring that was back on her finger. His head shot up and he looked her in the eye.

"Are you honestly engaged to him *again*?"

"Yes. Ellavorn and I are engaged again. It happened while we were in the other realm –."

"Other realm? What other realm?"

Arianna silently looked at Ellavorn, who raised an eyebrow at her.

"He was already under the sleeping curse when it all happened, Arianna."

"Can you all leave me and Joshua alone for a moment

while I fill him in on what happened after he was cursed?"

They all nodded and filed out the door.

Joshua looked at Arianna with an unreadable expression.

"What is the last thing that you remember, Joshua?"

"I left after you broke off our engagement. I was camping for the night in the woods, figuring out my next course of action. I saw a black flame and I have vague recollections of voices around me, but I couldn't place any of them. Only yours. And then one voice in particular, a woman, she would come in and talk to me. She kept saying that you had not returned yet. Where did you go, Arianna?"

"The night you were camping, that must be the night that the Dark Figure possessed you. He took over your body and came back here. He tried to use your body to get to me. He didn't take into account your stubbornness and gave it away. We were able to run him off, but you were left in that deep sleep. We brought you here while we tried to figure out how to wake you."

Joshua's face betrayed the fact that he was trying hard to remember all of these events.

"After we brought you here, Iron Demon and his pirates attacked the castle."

Joshua snapped to attention at that information.

"He came? He attacked? I am sorry. I thought it was a dream."

Arianna shook her head.

"It is forgiven. We evacuated everyone expect a few before he attacked and his men caught me."

Joshua's eyes grew large at that information.

"Ellavorn was among them. He was trying to help me. He tried to get me out, but the others found me before he could do that. Iron Demon forced me to abdicate, not knowing that the title of King and Queen are both cursed right now. The curse transferred to him. Ellavorn was able to convince the pirates that Iron Demon had broken the pact and they left."

"He must have been convincing in that. Iron Demon, while known for being ruthless, is also known for keeping his word."

Arianna nodded.

"He was able to convince them to leave."

"Where is Iron Demon now?"

"I'm getting to that part."

"After he abdicated, we put him in the dungeon. Adasser kept the elixir on hand to give him just enough to keep him alive, but unconscious. In the meantime, Adasser, Tanelia, Ellavorn and I crossed over to another realm."

"Another realm? Another realm? Arianna! This is absurd."

As Joshua said those words, one of the dragons outside made a noise and he froze.

"Arianna, what was that noise?"

"Well…I'm getting to that."

"Was that a *dragon*?"

"Ummmm, yes, yes, it was."

Joshua looked at her in utter horror.

"Please do not tell me that you brought a dragon back here!"

"Ok, I won't tell you that. We didn't bring a dragon back here."

Joshua looked at her suspiciously.

"We brought six, with about ten more on the way."

Joshua looked at her, utterly speechless as she smiled a sheepish smile at him.

"*YOU BROUGHT BACK SIX DRAGONS?*"

Chapter 40

The door banged open at the sound of Joshua's yelling and everyone came flooding back, this time joined by Adasser, Charlie and Armen.

"I see, or actually, heard, that you are awake, Captain Oakford," Adasser said. Tanelia stood behind him and snickered.

"You all allowed her to bring back dragons? *Dragons*?"

Améthystos's voice tinkled in Arianna's ears.

"This one is very dramatic. I can't tell if I like him or not."

Arianna laughed a short laugh, calling Joshua's attention to her.

"Oh, Arianna, I am so glad that you find this humorous. Dragons are dangerous. Why would you bring them here?"

"That is a part that she has not told us yet," Abigail chimed in.

"Yes, we will fill you all in now on the journey. Are Cecilia and Cassidy still awake? They may want to join in."

Charlie and Abigail shook their heads. "They climbed into their beds as soon as we showed them to their rooms," Abigail confirmed.

"That introduction will have to wait until tomorrow, I guess."

"Who are Cecilia and Cassidy?"

"Two of the wizards. Magus will be coming over with the rest of the dragons in a few days and, hopefully, Sumner will follow as well."

Joshua looked thoroughly confused. Everyone else waited for Arianna to start telling the story of their journey.

"Right, we crossed over into their realm and we were surrounded by woods. It took a few days for us to come across anybody. We fought wolves, but they turned out to be illusions that the wizards put into place for protection. Then, we came upon Roumpíni."

Joshua looked at her, "I'm sorry, who?"

"Roumpíni. He is a fire dragon. He is outside, guarding the castle now. We thought that he was going to attack us, and we fought back. Tanelia was about to kill him when Cecilia made herself known and stopped her. We followed her back, and found that the wizards had been breeding dragons."

"They were breeding them? On purpose?"

Arianna sighed.

"Yes, on purpose. To make a long story short, four of the

dragons pledged themselves to Adasser, Tanelia, Ellavorn and myself. We cannot leave them or they will die. If we die, they will as well. They had to come with us. They are going to help us in this fight."

Armen was the first to speak. "You brought dragons back to Eumetadotos to help us fight this evil thing?"

Arianna nodded.

"You said that they are pure right now, Arianna, but what if they turn?"

"They won't. They attach themselves to living beings that they feel are pure of heart. It is only if the one that they are bonded to is evil will they turn."

"And if those beings turn?"

Arianna went silent.

"I don't think that will happen, Father, unless you doubt our intentions?"

Armen's mouth snapped shut.

"It is not your intentions that I worry about, Ellavorn."

"The other two dragons have not bonded with anyone. We do not have to worry about that as of right now."

"They are loyal to Améthystos. She is their queen. Their

loyalty lies with her."

Améthystos's voice tinkled in her ears again.

"Show them the dagger. The elves will recognize it."

"There is something else as well. Améthystos is telling me to show you."

"Who is telling you what? I didn't hear anything. Arianna, are you hearing voices? That is never a good sign."

Arianna smiled, "No, Abigail. Améthystos is my bonded dragon. When a dragon bonds itself to you, you are able to communicate with them in your mind."

Abigail looked at her friend, uneasy. She looked to the other three, who all nodded in agreement, Tanelia rolling her eyes.

"Yes, you get to hear all of the dragon gossip, whether you want to or not."

"What will we do with them after we defeat this thing?" Adasser wanted to know.

"They will stay here."

"And the ones who are not bonded to anyone?"

"We will discuss what they wish to do after the final battle. I plan to leave that final decision up to them."

"And what of the wizards? What will they do?" Adasser asked.

"I intend to offer them the same deal. Should they choose to stay, they may. Should they choose to go back, they may with the offer to come back any time that they wish."

Charlie was uncharacteristically quiet through all of this.

"Arianna?"

"Yes, Charlie?"

"Will I get a dragon too?"

Arianna smiled. "If one of them choose you, you will. I cannot make any promises on their behalf. They have to make that decision. For themselves."

Charlie scratched his head and thought for a minute.

"I really hope that one of them chooses me! I want to ride a dragon!"

Arianna laughed.

"Well, even if they don't choose to bond to you, maybe one of them will allow you to ride on them."

Charlie pumped his fist in the air and yelled, "YESSSS!"

Arianna laughed again. "They have to make that decision,

Charlie. I cannot tell them what to do."

Charlie nodded, but she could see he was crossing his fingers and hoping that one of the dragons would choose him to bond to, or at least take him for a ride.

Armen looked at Charlie with fondness in his eyes as he stood up to speak. He looked at Ellavorn, Adasser, Tanelia and Arianna.

"Do you all know that there is a prophecy about this?"

Arianna sighed. "Of course there is. Why wouldn't there be?"

Armen looked at the four of them, the elves seemed to be in the dark as much as Arianna. "Of course, you would probably have not heard it. You usually do not hear of the prophecies that include yourself until they come to fruition. In this prophecy, the dragons return with the help of elves and humans. Those who have helped them, which I am assuming means the four of you, are called Dragon Masters."

Chapter 41

Everyone in the room looked around at each other in confusion, wondering what prophecy Armen was speaking of.

Armen spoke softly. *"The dragons shall return in the darkest hour. Mated to their counterparts, the Dragon Masters shall arise."*

He sighed and looked at Ellavorn, tears glistening. "I never would have guess that my own son would be a part of that particular prophecy."

"Armen, does the prophecy say anything else about The Dragon Masters and what we are supposed to do?"

Armen shook his head. "No. There was nothing else to that prophecy. No one had heard of Dragon Masters previously. We were always unsure of what it meant."

Améthystos's voice tinkled in Arianna's ears again.

"Dragon Masters simply means that the dragons have bonded themselves to you and that you shall master the knowledge of the dragons that we have and will continue to impart on you."

"Améthystos, did you know about this prophecy?"

"I know of all of the prophecies, child."

"Why wouldn't you tell me?"

Her laugh tinkled in Arianna's ears again.

"It wasn't time to tell you. However, you could have looked for the answer yourself."

Arianna sighed, "I never thought of reading your thoughts. I don't even know how."

"Just concentrate, child. It will come."

"Ari? Are you ok?" Abigail sounded worried.

Arianna's attention snapped back to the room around her.

"I'm sorry. I was speaking with Améthystos, who apparently knew about this particular prophecy. She just didn't seem to think it was important to share," Arianna huffed.

The laughter tinkled in her ears again.

"What do you mean, you were speaking with the dragon?" It was Armen's turn to be confused.

Arianna smirked. She, at last, had information that Armen didn't.

"When a dragon bonds himself or herself to you, you can speak telepathically to each other. We can read each other's minds, and communicate."

Armen looked astonished.

"How is that possible?"

Améthystos's voice tinkled in Arianna's ears again, but this time, it sounded bored.

"This elf thinks that he knows everything about dragons, doesn't he?"

"He knows more about the dragons that lived here than most others do."

"He doesn't know everything."

"I don't think that he assumes that he does. Be nice."

Améthystos huffed. "Please explain to him the mind links. You may also wish to let him know of the dagger. It is time to reveal that it is in your possession. He may find that information useful."

Arianna had almost forgotten about the Stiléto me fteró drákou.

"I will tell them all now."

Arianna turned her attention back to the room.

"Were you speaking with the dragon again?" Armen inquired.

Arianna nodded. "Yes, and she requested that I explain what is happening between the dragons and ourselves. But, first,

Ellavorn, will you please retrieve the package from my chambers?"

Ellavorn smiled, nodded and left the room to retrieve the dagger as Arianna began to explain the mind links. Arianna walked to the window, and Améthystos flew up and looked into the window as she spoke.

"Dragons are a lot more complex than I ever knew. Of course, I had never seen them until we crossed realms, but from what I had been told, they were violent creatures. This is simply not true. Améthystos told me that dragons can see into your heart and can tell what you hold in there. The dragon decides if you are a match for them and if they will bond themselves to you."

She looked at the dragon at the window for reassurance. Améthystos nodded and she continued.

"The dragon then does a bonding ritual, which these four have done to bond themselves to us. Once you complete that ritual by laying your hand on their head, it opens the mind link between you. You can read each other's thoughts. You have access to their memories, and they have access to yours."

"You can read each other's minds?" Abigail seemed flabbergasted by this information.

"Yes. You can. It is how we communicate. Dragons can't talk." Améthystos's laugh tinkled in Arianna's ears again.

Arianna continued. "When dragons are hatched, they have the colored scales that you see on the ones who accompanied us home. They are beautiful and gemstone colored. If the being that they bond themselves to turns evil, or if the unbonded dragon turns evil, the scales will turn dark. The dragons of our lure had all turned. There was no good left in them."

Arianna turned to Armen, Adasser and Tanelia.

"The dragons that were slain all those years ago, they were beyond redemption. You had no choice but to get rid of them. There was one good dragon left. Aldore had found her. She gave him 4 eggs to take with him when he was exiled. Those four eggs are where these dragons came from. Under the care of the wizard family, they have grown in number and none of the dragons that we have met have any evil in their hearts that we have seen."

Tanelia snorted, "Except the Flower Stomper."

Arianna laughed. "Yes, Roumpíni is mischievous, but he is not evil."

"I'm pretty sure that Keandra would disagree with you on that point."

They both laughed while Abigail, Charlie and Armen looked on in utter confusion.

"What happened over there?" Abigail asked.

Tanelia smiled a small smile. "I've come to realize that not all humans are bad. Arianna and I may not always see eye to eye on everything, but we have come to realize that we are not as different as we thought we were."

Arianna smiled and added, "We have actually come to like each other quite a lot."

The looks of absolute astonishment on everyone's faces made both of them laugh.

"Back to the matter at hand. These dragons that have pledged themselves to us did so because they saw the goodness in our hearts and they wish to help in our fight and we desperately need that help."

"Do any more dragons intend to bond themselves to anyone else?"

"I am unsure of that. The bond is not something that they take lightly. If a dragon is separated from the being that it bonds itself to, that dragon will die."

"What if the dragon dies? Will you die?" Joshua spoke up for the first time.

Arianna shook her head, "No. The dragons are the more vulnerable party, which is why it is a privilege for them to choose you."

"A privilege? Arianna, they are dangerous creatures!"

"Joshua, enough! I have explained to you that they are not dangerous unless they turn."

"And what if they do?"

"The ones that have bonded themselves to us will not."

"What of the others? What if they turn?"

Améthystos's voice tinkled again. "If any of them turn, it will mean certain death for them. I will personally see to that. I will not stand for evil among my dragons. I promise you."

"Améthystos gives her word that if any of them start to turn, that she will deal with them herself."

"Meaning?"

"Certain death."

The answer seemed to appease Joshua for the moment, although, Arianna could sense that he was not done with this argument. She decided to get back to the subject of the dragon bonds.

"Améthystos, Zafeíri, Ellavorn and I went on a walk the night before we left Cassidy and Cecilia's home. We were able to visit the grave of the brave dragon that gave her life for her eggs in order for the dragon bloodline to continue."

Arianna looked at the door as Ellavorn walked back in, carrying a white fabric bag. He handed it to her.

"I came back from that walk with a souvenir."

She pulled the dagger out and she heard Armen gasp.

"The Stiléto Me Fteró Drákou!"

Chapter 42

From the doorway, Cassidy's awed voice said, "Can it be, after all of these years, the Stiléto Me Fteró Drákou? You found it?"

Arianna startled and turned towards the door where both Cassidy and Cecilia were standing with their eyes on the dagger. She nodded.

"Améthystos and Zafeíri took us to the dragon's grave and it presented itself to me before we began our journey to visit Magus."

Cassidy looked at her and quietly said, "But, why didn't you tell me that you had this in your possession?"

Améthystos's voice tinkled in her ears, "Go ahead, child, tell him that I asked you not to."

Arianna averted her eyes and told him, "Améthystos wanted to keep it quiet for the time being."

"I see. Did the dragon think that I would steal it from you?"

The tinkling voice rang through Arianna's ear again.

"Yes. He would have."

Arianna sighed and nodded her head. She felt apprehensive about being put in the middle of the argument.

Cassidy's face darkened slightly.

"Did she tell you why she thinks that I would have taken it?"

"Because he would want to use the dagger for his own selfish purposes, child."

"What purposes are those, Améthystos? I can't make him guess on the answers. Besides, I would like to know this information as well."

"Because he knows that the Stiléto Me Fteró Drákou can be used to free him from his bonds and he would be able to practice magic again."

Arianna gasped and looked at Cassidy.

"So, she told you? That the dagger can be used to unbind you from doing magic."

Joshua groaned from his bad, from which he still had not gotten up.

"Arianna, let me get this straight, you brought back *six* dragons *and* a bound wizard?"

"I did what I had to do for the safety of my kingdom, Joshua."

"Are you sure about that? Do you know how dangerous one

of those options is on its own, let alone *both*?"

"Joshua, once again your listening skills, or lack thereof, never cease to amaze me. Did you not hear me explain the dragon lore? The dragons are on *our* side this time. They will not harm us."

Joshua huffed.

"I am growing extremely weary of your insufferable attitude, Captain Oakford."

A small spark jolted from Arianna's fingertip. She shook her hands in the air and took a few deep breaths so that she didn't lose control.

Joshua looked as though he had been slapped in the face by her scolding.

Ellavorn stifled a laugh.

"Listen, Captain Oakford, I wouldn't put up a fight with her. At this point, she would probably win in a duel. She does have powers, and, even though they are better than they were, they are still not completely stable."

"I didn't ask you, Elf."

"Enough! Captain Oakford, you will not show disrespect to my fiancé again!"

"Right, I forgot, you're engaged again."

"I think it would be best if you did not forget that."

Another small spark flew from Arianna's fingertips. Joshua eyed them with contempt on his face. Arianna sighed and sat down in one of the chairs. He put her head in her hands, breathing deeply and trying to calm herself from Joshua's verbal attacks.

Ellavorn stood next to her, his hand on her shoulder. His touch seemed to calm her almost instantly. She covered his hand with hers and smiled up at him before looking around the room.

"Can all of you please give me a moment alone with Captain Oakford? I believe that there are some things that need to be discussed."

Everyone started to leave the room, including Ellavorn. Arianna squeezed his hand and said, "Please stay, this involves you too."

Abigail was the last to leave. She turned to look back. Her gaze lingered on Joshua, then shot to Arianna, Ellavorn and back to Joshua. She sighed and left the room and Arianna did not miss her actions. Abigail shut the door behind her and Arianna turned to face Joshua with a look that held all of her anger. Joshua let a look of fear cross his face for a split second, before putting on his stony façade again.

"Captain Oakford, I have told you in the past that you need to learn to stand down when I say to stand down. This war we are facing is unlike any other that you have ever faced. The battles consist of magic and magical beings. If we are to make it out of this war with minimal casualties, you must trust me."

"Arianna, you do not have experience with war or battles of any kind. I do."

"But, I have fought off the Dark Figure multiple times now. I am learning my enemy and its weaknesses. We need you on board for when the attacks come again and he brings it in numbers. Not all of us have the ability to fight with powers or magic. We need your help to train them and guide them. But, we cannot do that if you are going to continue to push back on everything that I say and do."

Joshua thought about this for a moment.

"I understand. I will train those who need to be trained."

"I think that Tanelia and Adasser will be able to help with that," Ellavorn volunteered.

Joshua gritted his teeth.

"Actually, I think that is a good idea, Ellavorn," Arianna said.

Joshua looked incredulous at the suggestion.

"But, I –"

"You have seen them fight, Captain. They can teach you some things and you can teach them. One thing I learned on this journey is that we can learn from each other, put our differences aside and work together."

Joshua scoffed, but his voice softened.

"So, you are back to calling me Captain Oakford?"

"Well, with the way you have been acting lately, I saw it fit to move back to a professional level."

Joshua sighed.

"I apologize for my behavior as of late. I can assure you that I will work on improving that."

"Thank you. Now, I asked Ellavorn to stay so that we can discuss the issue among the three of us and come to an understanding. Ellavorn and I are engaged again. This time, we will be married."

Joshua started to make a face, but caught himself.

"You must respect that, Joshua. Ellavorn is going to be the king and my husband."

Joshua grimaced and looked away for a moment.

"Why wouldn't you come back when I found you? She

wanted you then. You wouldn't leave the pirate."

"I desperately wanted to. I wanted nothing more than to come back here to Arianna and act as though nothing happened. I couldn't. I had to stay with Iron Demon. I knew that he planned to attack Eumetadotos, but I didn't know when or how. I knew that I had to stay so that I could work from the inside to help Arianna and I did. I would not change that decision at all."

Joshua nodded, still looking at the wall.

"Captain Oakford, I did not stay away because I did not love her anymore. I stayed away because I love her more than anything. I would sacrifice everything for Arianna, even if it means that I have to stay away for a short amount of time so that I can protect her in my way."

Joshua said softly, "I love her too."

"I know that you do. I respect your feelings towards her and I will not do anything to flaunt our love in front of you. I know how it feels to lose Arianna. I lost her once myself."

Joshua finally turned to look at them and a single tear trailed down his cheek. He swiftly brushed it away and put on a stoic face again.

"I will respect your engagement and I will resume my duties of Captain of the Royal Guard with a more professional attitude."

He turned to Arianna.

"Can we still be on friendly terms? I know I lost you as a partner, but I do not wish to lose you altogether as a friend as well. You are important to me."

Arianna smiled.

"You are important to me too, Joshua. You have been a good friend to me in the past and, as long as you can come to terms that I am different now, we can be good friends again."

Joshua nodded, but then noticed that the door was open ajar. He saw a flash of light blue before the door clicked shut again.

"Someone was listening in," he said as he jumped from the bed and ran to the door.

He jerked the door open and looked both ways down that hall, but there was no one to be seen. He looked back at Arianna and Ellavorn, both of whom were already on their feet, in defensive stances, and motioned with his head for them to come with him.

"We should probably split up. Check all of the rooms. They couldn't have gone very far."

Arianna opened the door to her chambers and found

Abigail sitting in a chair, facing the window, tears streaming down her face and falling on to her light blue skirts. The sight broke Arianna's heart.

"I think I found her,"

She called to the other two, who came running.

"I've got this. You two go make friends."

Arianna made a shoo-ing motion with her hands before shutting the door in their bewildered faces.

She turned back to her best friend, sat on the bed and said, "OK, Abigail, spill. What is going on?"

Abigail put her head on the windowsill and began to sob.

Chapter 43

Arianna's heart broke more than she ever thought possible, watching her best friend in so much pain. She went over and threw her arms around her, hugging her tightly.

"Abigail, please tell me what is wrong?"

"Oh, Ari, I'm so sorry. I didn't mean to eavesdrop. I couldn't help it."

"Abigail, I don't care if you were eavesdropping. That can't possibly be why you are this distraught. What is happening?"

"I – I – I love him, Ari."

"You love who?"

Abigail drew a shaky breath.

"Captain Oakford. I'm sorry. I tried not to, but I just couldn't help it. I didn't want to. It just happened."

"Abigail, stop. I am not angry. You do not have to explain anything to me. I know how love works. It is strange and mysterious and wonderful at the same time."

"I am a fool, Ari. Captain Oakford would never notice me. He was engaged to you. You are the queen. I am just a handmaiden."

"Excuse me? You *are not* just a handmaiden. You are my *best* friend and he would be a fool to not notice how special you are. Abigail, it was you that took care of him while I was gone, am I right?"

Abigail nodded, her sobs slowed, but the tears still kept coming.

"I don't think that he realizes how big of a thank you he owes to you for that."

"Please do not say anything to anyone, Ari. I don't think that I can handle that rejection."

"You have my word that I will not say anything unless you feel ready to confess, but I will leave that to you."

"Thank you."

"Now, I am sure that you are hungry. I am starving. Why don't we go see what is for dinner. I take it we have food in the castle, am I correct?"

Abigail nodded.

"We do, however, Armen isn't such a great cook and I am afraid that he was going down to make supper. We didn't feel safe bringing anyone back to cook or clean. I had been taking care of keeping things tidy, as there are not many staying here."

"Abigail, thank you for taking over while I was gone. You

made the right decision to not bring anyone back. I do not know what the Dark Figure is plotting and I do not want more people than have to be in harm's way."

Abigail smiled and hugged her friend.

"How about we go down and get something to eat? I'm sure that we can figure out something to make Armen's food a bit more...palpable?"

The two of them made their way down to the kitchens, where they heard more yelling.

"I have been doing the cooking since everyone has been gone. I know what I am doing!" Armen's voice echoed against the walls.

"I pity everyone who has eaten the food that you have been cooking!" Tanelia's voice was just as loud.

"I don't think that this chicken is even edible!"

Arianna and Abigail heard a "Thwack" and a yell.

"How dare you! That was a perfectly good piece of chicken!"

This was followed by Tanelia's laughter.

Arianna and Abigail looked at each other and turned the corner to see Armen, red-faced with anger and Tanelia, doubled over in laughter.

Arianna cleared her throat, making both stand up straight and look over at her.

"What's going on in here?" She asked, trying not to laugh.

Both elves started stammering, and Arianna's eyes found the piece of chicken that Tanelia had apparently thrown at the wall. It was still stuck there. She bit her lip to keep from laughing and took a deep breath.

"Armen, I appreciate all of the work that you have done to keep everyone fed. Perhaps you might wish to take the night off and allow Tanelia to cook for everyone tonight?"

She shot Tanelia a pointed look, which Tanelia acknowledged and kept quiet.

"Arianna, I don't mind cooking for everyone. I quite enjoyed it."

"I am sure that you did. However, I think that Tanelia has something in mind for that chicken. How about allowing her to make that while you take a break for the night? I am sure that she can handle it for the night."

Armen sighed. "As you wish."

Armen left the room, and Arianna turned back to Abigail and Tanelia and all three burst into laughter.

"Tanelia, can you save that chicken?"

"I believe that I can."

"OK, great, get to work. Just please don't use the piece that you stuck to the wall? I prefer my chicken without the added minerals?"

All three burst into laughter again as Tanelia peeled the chicken from the wall and threw it in the garbage pail.

"What did he do to it to make it stick to the wall like that?" Arianna inquired.

"Ari, you just don't want to know. Tanelia, thank you for saving us from another one of his disasters."

"You're welcome. I wonder why he just didn't bring in someone from The Forest Glen to cook."

The other two shrugged and all three burst into laughter again.

"OK, you two, out of the kitchen. I will have this prepared in no time."

Tanelia shooed them out of the kitchen and they made their way to the hall, where they found Adasser and Armen sitting and talking in hushed voices. They were obviously discussing something very important. They also found Ellavorn and Joshua sitting together and laughing and talking as though they were old friends. Arianna sighed and looked at Abigail, who was making dreamy eyes at Joshua.

They walked over to where Ellavorn and Joshua sat and asked, "Are these seats taken?"

"No, please, sit down."

As they sat, Cassidy and Cecilia entered the room. Arianna waved them over and they took two of the remaining three seats, awkwardly.

Cassidy looked around the room, curiously.

"I have always wondered what the castle looked like. Every room is just magnificent."

Arianna smiled.

"When we defeat this Dark Figure and everything can return to normal, you must stay and see it in all of its glory."

Cassidy smile and Cecilia looked as though she were going to jump out of her seat.

Cassidy chuckled.

"We will discuss that when the time comes."

Cecilia gave a disappointed face, but snapped out of it fairly quickly.

"I can show you around after supper, if you like," Abigail offered.

Cecilia's face brightened.

"Really? I would love that. I have dreamed of coming here all my life. I can't believe it is coming true."

Abigail smiled.

"Of course. I know all about the castle."

"Not more than me!"

Charlie appeared at Abigail's elbow and they all laughed.

"You're right, Charlie. No one knows more about the castle than you do."

Charlie beamed.

"Can I show Cecilia around too?"

"Well, of course. I wouldn't deprive our guest of the best tour guide that the castle has to offer!"

With that, Tanelia came in with plates on a rolling cart. She grabbed a plate for herself and went to sit with Adasser and Armen.

"I cooked it, you can all help yourselves."

Arianna laughed as she looked around at all of her friends

and she knew, deep down that everything was going to be alright, at least for the time being.

Chapter 44

The next few days passed in a blue of everyone getting to know each other and training, both magical and non-magical. Joshua taught everyone, including Arianna and the elves how to use a sword. Tanelia taught them all how to throw daggers. Adasser gave Arianna one on one training on how to cultivate her magic.

"You are doing very well, Arianna. Very well indeed."

"Thank you, Adasser. I am trying my best. Although, I don't think that it is good enough to defeat the Dark Figure yet."

Adasser smiled.

"All in time. All in time. You have not yet reached your full potential."

"I fear that I never will. I feel as though I keep trying and coming up short."

"That is ok. You are learning. You have come so far so fast. Of course, I would not have expected any less from my granddaughter, and the Prophesized One."

Arianna smiled and shook her head.

"I am unsure of how to be the Prophesized One. I mean, all my life, I've just been me and all of the sudden, I was thrown into the spotlight to be destined to save everyone. It's just a lot all at once."

"Well, lucky for you, you have a wonderful support system," he gestured to the group that had begun hand-to-hand combat training.

Arianna looked at all of them and smiled, realizing that she did, indeed, have a fantastic support system to help her. She looked at back at Adasser with a renewed sense of confidence.

"Adasser, I will defeat this figure. I will save my people."

Adasser smiled. "I know you will. Now, we should get in there and train. Captain Oakford will be disappointed that we are late."

They walked into the room and picked up the sparring swords. Arianna noticed that a few of the guards were training today as well. She noticed Dustin Granitious sparring with Armen. He noticed her and nodded. She smiled and nodded back.

"Well, it's about time the two of you showed up," Joshua said, a little bit of irritation in his voice.

"Yes, training ran a little over today," Adasser explained.

"Very well, the two of you will be sparring partners. Everyone else has already paired up."

"We have never sparred before," noted Arianna.

"I won't hurt you," joked Adasser.

"I know. I won't let you."

The two of them got into the sparring positions that Joshua had taught them and started sparring. Arianna seemed to second guess Adasser's every move. She blocked and jabbed flawlessly. Adasser was surprised at how well she could keep up.

Joshua watched in amazement as Arianna and Adasser were locked in a sort of ballet of sword fighting. He knew that Arianna had picked it up quickly, but even he was amazed at just how quickly.

"Time is up. Swords down."

Everyone stopped fighting and went to put their swords away.

"Arianna, not you," Joshua said while picking up a sword of his own.

Everyone turned to watch what was happening. Arianna was confused. Joshua had never singled her out like this before.

"Arianna, you need the most training since you are destined to fight this...*thing*...on your own. You need to train harder. Come here. You and I are going to spar."

Arianna looked around and then back at Joshua with fear and confusion on her face. Joshua was known for being fierce with a sword. It was the reason that he held the position that he did. He saw the emotions on her face and laughed.

"I am not going to hurt you. You have to be on the top of your game if you are going to have a chance to win this."

"But, she can use her powers," Cassidy said.

"Yes, she can. However, she needs to train in hand-to-hand combat as well in case she is in a situation where her powers will not be the best choice of weapon."

"How would that not be the best choice of weapon?"

Joshua twirled his sword in circles, moving gracefully around the room, getting closer to Cassidy. When he was close enough, he grabbed Cassidy and held him from behind.

"Now, what would you do to get out of this with magic? From what I have seen, magic would harm both of us in this position."

Cassidy bowed his head in surrender.

"You are correct. Magic and Elven Powers would cause damage to both of us in this situation. However, how would you get out of this situation?"

Joshua grinned and showed him a secret pocket in his armor where he kept a small, but very sharp dagger.

"With this. I have only had to use it once," he said sadly, as he stole a glance at Arianna, remembering the day that her parents were murdered. Joshua still considered it his ultimate failure.

"Well, that would surely cause some damage, now wouldn't it?"

"Captain Oakford, can I have a dagger too? I promise to be really careful with it!" Charlie asked.

Joshua ruffled his hair.

"Not at this time, Charlie. You aren't skilled enough yet. I don't want to give you something that could hurt you."

Charlie huffed, and muttered under his breath, "I bet I could use that dagger the best."

Joshua stifled a smile.

"Now, Arianna, come over here and let's test your skills."

Arianna approached and they started their sparring match. She was able to easily block and avoid all of Joshua's attacks. She fiercely attacked back, surprising him with how skilled she had become in a short amount of time. Everyone watched in awe as Arianna held her own with Joshua.

"That is enough training for today. You are doing remarkably well."

"It must be the fighter bloodlines in you," Tanelia piped up.

Arianna smiled, "That and the great trainers I have all around."

After they all had put their swords away, they all walked down to the kitchen to figure out something to eat. Armen tried to lead the way, but was stopped by everyone Ellavorn.

"Father, you are good at many things, but cooking is not your strong suit."

Armen looked indignantly at his son as everyone else averted their eyes.

"I have been making the food here since we evacuated the castle. Everyone loves my cooking."

Abigail and Charlie wandered off, trying to escape any line of questioning that may be thrown their way.

"I don't doubt that you gave it your best try, Father, however, I don't think that they really enjoyed your cooking."

Armen looked around the room for Abigail and Charlie, but found that they had both left the room. He made a sulky face and huffed.

"Well, fine then. Who do you think could do a better job?"

"Well, Tanelia did a great job last night. I heard that the

chicken that you made actually stuck to the wall?" Ellavorn hesitantly brought up Armen's culinary failure from the night before while trying not to laugh.

Armen refused to answer and stormed out of the room.

"I guess I should go apologize to my father. The rest of you can thank me later. Tanelia, I'm sorry for volunteering you for that task."

Tanelia rolled her eyes and nodded.

"I guess I should be glad that we don't have to suffer through another Armen Disaster Dinner. If you see Abigail and the kid, can you please send them back in? I am going to need their help."

Ellavorn nodded and turned to leave the room as Abigail and Charlie tried to sneak back in.

"I was going to come looking for the two of you before going to find my father. Tanelia needs your help."

Charlie jumped up and down and ran back into the kitchen, stopping suddenly when he realized that he had forgotten that he was afraid of Tanelia. He eyed her suspiciously and she pointed to some vegetables that were left on the counter. Charlie grinned and grabbed his knife and started cutting them up.

Abigail walked over and began to help Tanelia season the

meat that was on the counter while Arianna and Adasser left to freshen up.

"How is this food staying so fresh?" Tanelia wanted to know.

"Oh, Armen has elves bring fresh food over to us every day."

"Wait, he has them bring the food, but he insisted on subjecting you to his cooking? Every day?"

Abigail gave Tanelia a look.

"Every. Day."

Tanelia shook her head and laughed.

"That sounds like our King. He's very stubborn. Much like our Prince. Although, neither will never admit that they are stubborn."

Abigail laughed. "It's ok, Ari is the same, but don't tell her I said that."

Tanelia laughed, a sound that took both Abigail and Charlie by surprise.

"What? I laugh."

Both of them looked at her in awe. Neither had really heard her laugh before.

"What?" She asked again.

"It's just that when you left, you hated us because we are human. You wouldn't dare give us the time of day. Now, you are working in the kitchen with us and…laughing. We are just not used to this."

"Yeah, well, Arianna has a way of growing on you…like a fungus…but in the best way possible. It really is hard to hate her, isn't it?"

Abigail smiled and nodded.

Charlie continued to stare at Tanelia in fear.

"Chop those veggies!" Tanelia cried.

Charlie began chopping as though his life depended on it, making both Abigail and Tanelia laugh.

Tanelia turned to Abigail.

"My view of humans seems to be softening some. I still do not understand your mortality, nor would I wish to taint my bloodline with it, but humans themselves aren't all bad. This journey with Arianna has opened my eyes to how we are alike in as many ways as we are different. I am glad for that journey. I've never really had a friend before. I have begun to think of Arianna as just that, a friend."

Abigail's eyes grew wide.

"You've never had a friend? What about Adasser or Ellavorn?"

"Adasser was always more like a father to me and Ellavorn, well, we were a couple for a long time. I've never had a friend like Arianna…or you."

Abigail smiled. "You want to be my friend?"

"Possibly, as long as you don't get all girly and start squealing and stuff."

"I promise."

"OK, good. Now, let's get this lunch together and feed everyone. I am sure that they are all starving. I know I am. Captain Oakford is a pretty good instructor."

Abigail blushed at the mention of Joshua.

"Yeah, he's the best at what he does."

Tanelia noticed the blush, but said nothing. Just made a mental note of it as they finished preparing the lunch feast for everyone, laughing and talking as they cooked.

Chapter 45

Back in the hall, everyone had gathered for lunch. Cassidy and Cecilia seemed to be growing more at ease with everyone else and Cassidy took a seat with Adasser and Armen. Cecilia and Arianna were sitting at a table with Ellavorn and Joshua. It looked as though the ladies were getting along, however, the men sat in silence, seemingly not comfortable with each other.

Just as Abigail and Tanelia were pushing the cart with lunch into the hall, the castle began to shake. Everyone looked at each other and Cecilia jumped up and ran to the window with a huge smile on her face.

"Grandfather! He's coming!"

Cassidy smiled and walked slowly to the window as well. His gait showed less enthusiasm than his daughter's.

"Ah, yes, he is with the rest of the dragons." They saw about nine dragons filing through the portal, one by one.

Arianna had joined them at the window.

"Why are they all coming through one portal? Can't they all use their scales and come through all at once?"

Cecilia shook her head, "No, they need someone to activate

the scales for them."

Arianna nodded.

"Well, I think that we should go and greet our guests, what do you think?"

Cecilia ran out of the room in the direction of the door.

The rest of the group followed her outside. When they got there, the dragons had lined up, shoulder to shoulder, facing everyone. Cecilia kept straining her neck, looking for her grandfather, and hoping to see her brother come through. Her grandfather, riding on Ydátinos, was the last one through and the portal sealed itself behind him.

Cecilia looked crestfallen when she didn't see her brother riding on any of the dragons. Cassidy noticed and put his arm around his daughter to try to comfort her.

Magus dismounted Ydátinos with a flourish and went to Cecilia and Cassidy.

"I tried to get the boy to come with me. He flat out refused. He kept one of the dragons with him in case he changes his mind. Although, I do not think that he will. He is stubborn in his hatred."

"Sumner has always been a tad hard-headed," Cassidy said.

Magus raised his eyebrows at his son. "Reminds me of his father."

Cassidy opened his mouth to say something, but through better of it and turned and walked away.

Arianna approached the newcomer with Armen, Adasser and Ellavorn.

"Magus, thank you for coming and bringing the dragons with you. Let me introduce Armen, the Elven King and Ellavorn's father. I trust that you are hungry? We were just about to sit down to lunch. Please, join us."

Magus nodded and they all went back inside to eat lunch. While they were walking, Arianna opened the mind link with Améthystos.

"The rest of the dragons are here. Could you please bring them to where you are all staying?"

Améthystos's voice rang in her ears. "We are on our way. It is about time they got here. We need some rest from patrolling the castle. Reinforcements are greatly appreciated."

Arianna smiled and continued the walk back to the hall with her friends.

Abigail was the first to approach her.

"Ari, those dragons…there are so many of them. Can we trust them all?"

Arianna smiled and touched her friend's shoulder.

"I would not have brought them here if I did not trust them. Améthystos has given me her word that we have nothing to worry about."

Abigail continued to look worried.

"I just have never heard of a dragon that could be trusted."

"I never had either, until I met these dragons. They are quite unlike any dragons from the history that we have been told."

Abigail nodded. "They are quite beautiful."

"They are, aren't they? Their scales just glisten in the sun. It is quite stunning."

"But, they can be quite dangerous if they do turn on us."

Arianna stopped and turned to Abigail, putting both hands on both of her shoulders this time and looking her friend in the eye.

"I promise you, Abigail, if any of them show any sign of turning, it will be dealt with immediately. I promise."

Abigail nodded and they walked back to the hall.

When they entered the hall, everyone had begun eating so they each took a plate and loaded it up with food and started walking to their table. They saw that Magus had joined Cassidy, Armen and Adasser at their table. They noticed that Magus had a jar in the middle of the table.

"Ari, what is in that jar? It looks strange."

"It's dragon's blood."

Abigail looked at her in horror.

"Dragon's blood? Why would they save that? Why would they bring that here?"

Arianna smiled.

"Dragon's blood is quite useful. It can heal quicker than Ellavorn can. It is quite remarkable."

Cecilia smiled.

"It has so many more benefits than just healing properties."

Their table had grown full with Ellavorn, Joshua, Tanelia, Charlie and Cecilia already at the table. Arianna and Abigail both sat at the table, and everyone grew interested to hear what Cecilia had to say.

"Their blood can also increase your strength for a short amount of time. Your magical abilities as well. I'm sure that Grandfather is telling them about the benefits now."

Abigail looked concerned. "How do you get the blood? You don't hurt them, do you?"

Cecilia smiled. "Of course not. Most dragons are quite clumsy, especially Roumpíni. When they are wounded, we gather what we can before they heal. They heal quite quickly, so we have to be quite fast in order to gather it. We had a lot in stock, but lately, it has been dwindling somehow. We haven't been able to figure it out."

"Would the dragons be taking it back?" Arianna asked

"No, once the blood is shed, they have no use for it. I don't know why they would want it back."

"You said that their blood gives you strength, at least temporarily, correct?"

Cecilia nodded, thoughtfully.

"That is correct."

"What if someone is stealing it for that reason?"

"But, who would be using it? It is not like any of us were doing anything that would require more strength."

Arianna thought about it for a moment.

"It just doesn't make any sense."

"I know, it has been perplexing us all for months."

Arianna's eyes snapped up.

"This has been happening for months?"

"Yes."

Just then, the ground began to shake again. They all looked at each other and ran to the window as another portal opened and a dragon stepped through, Sumner riding on his back.

"Sumner!" Cecilia squealed and ran outside to meet her twin.

Arianna and Abigail looked at each other in confusion.

"Ari, I thought that Magus said he wasn't coming."

"He did. Maybe Sumner changed his mind. Be careful with him, Abigail. He doesn't like Eumetadotos. He hates anyone from here."

Abigail nodded.

"Should we go meet him?"

"I will go. You stay here."

Arianna turned to Ellavorn and Joshua.

"The two of you stay here with her. I will meet Sumner outside."

They nodded and took Abigail back to her seat. She hesitantly went with them, watching Arianna leave the room.

Arianna made her way to the front and found Sumner with Cassidy and Magus.

"Welcome, Sumner. I hope that you find yourself comfortable during your stay."

Sumner grunted at her and turned away.

"Would you care to join us for lunch? We have just started."

Sumner grunted again, but followed Cecilia back into the hall, where he grabbed a plate, piled it with food and sat with Cecilia, glaring at everyone at the table. Cecilia introduced everyone, thrilled that her brother had decided to join them, although he made the rest of the table uncomfortable.

Sumner ate in silence, glaring at everyone as he ate. He and Cecilia finished their lunch before everyone else.

"Cecilia, Sumner may have the room next to yours. Would you care to show him the way?"

"Absolutely! Sumner, come, I will show you the way!"

He grunted again as he rose to go after her.

"Well, isn't he just a ray of sunshine?" Abigail retorted.

"Get used to it. He's always like this," Arianna responded, shaking her head.

"Actually, he was a lot more polite this encounter than he has been in the past," Ellavorn spoke up. He, Arianna and Tanelia chuckled.

Just then, the room began to shake, and a shrill voice rang out through the hall.

"So, you're back, Little Queenie? It took you long enough. I have to say, tapping the Wizard and bringing back dragons, what a nice touch. You can call for all of the reinforcements you want to, but you will not defeat me!"

"Abigail, Charlie, get out of here, quickly! Go out the back way!"

Abigail and Charlie ran to the back of the room as Arianna and everyone else got into defensive stances, facing the door.

"Quite foolish of you to send them straight into my clutches, Queenie."

Arianna froze as she heard Abigail and Charlie both scream at the same time.

"No!"

She slowly turned to see the Dark Figure standing there, its arms both outstretched and Abigail and Charlie both suspended in the air. It seemed as though it were squeezing them both around the middle, and hard.

"No! Let them go!" Arianna screamed and she let out a ball of light that struck the Dark Figure in the shoulder, forcing it to lose grip on Charlie, who took the opportunity to run to Arianna. She pushed him under the table.

"Charlie, the first chance you get, you run!"

Charlie nodded and watched in fear from under the table.

The Dark Figure pushed Abigail in front of itself to use as a shield as it moved closer. Arianna was too scared to attack so as not to hurt her friend.

Just then, a dagger flew through the air towards the Dark Figure. It threw its free hand up, melting the dagger.

Dustin Granitious yelled out in anger, "That was my best dagger!"

The Dark Figure turned toward Dustin and started advancing.

"Fool! You cannot harm me with a mere mortal dagger."

Another ball of light hit the Dark Figure, this time, it was Adasser that had thrown it. This seemed to anger it and it changed its course and headed towards Adasser. Abigail was still struggling and screaming as it moved around the room. Arianna felt helpless watching her friend so scared and in pain. She didn't know what to do.

"Use your powers, child," Améthystos's voice tinkled in her ears again.

"I can't! What if I hit Abigail?"

"You have to take the chance, child. It will not let her go unless you make it."

Arianna sent another ball of light directly at the Dark Figure's shoulder, making direct contact. It screamed and dropped Abigail, who fell to the ground and passed out in pain.

The Dark Figure looked around the room quickly and saw the dragon's blood. It made a mad dash to the jar, grabbing it as it went past and ran into the hall.

"Joshua, get Abigail to safety! I am going after the Dark Figure!"

"Arianna, no! I will go with you."

"Do not argue with me! Get her and Charlie out of here and somewhere safe!"

Joshua ran to Abigail, lifting her in his arms. Her face was deathly pale and her breathing very shallow.

He looked at Ellavorn, "Ellavorn, please, help her!"

Ellavorn looked at her and said, "Let's get her to her room. I can help her there."

Ellavorn grabbed Charlie and they ran out of the room to safety.

Chrissy White

Chapter 46

Arianna ran faster than she ever thought possible. The blood strummed in her ears, drowning out her footsteps. The Dark Figure will pay for this. It killed her parents, and now, hurt her best friend. She was not going to let it get away.

It turned and ran down into the dungeons and she followed.

"Améthystos, it is heading to the dungeons."

"I know, child, I can detect him. I will be ready to help."

Arianna was confused, but didn't have time to think. She kept running, trying to catch up. She ran down the stairs, going deeper into the dungeons, down to where they had held Iron Demon until just a few days ago.

It was quite dark, and it was deathly quiet. Arianna noticed the torches on the walls and quietly lit them all at once with her powers. She heard a footstep echo, but she couldn't figure out where it had come from.

She looked all around her when she heard Adasser and Armen calling her name.

She got into defensive mode and yelled back to them, "Stay back! I have to fight this battle on my own!"

"Arianna, you need reinforcements. We can help you!"

"Do not allow them to come down, child. It will use them to hurt you."

"No! Stay where you are! I have to fight this on my own."

"Arianna, you need help!" Adasser came down the stairs and ran towards Arianna, a ball of black magic flew at him, hitting him and sending him into the stone wall, hitting his head hard and knocking him to the ground.

"No! Adasser!" Arianna screamed and carefully went to him. He was bleeding profusely from his head wound and was stunned by the blow, but he was ok.

"Get out of here. I can't risk you or anyone else getting hurt. I have to fight this battle on my own. It is trying to hurt you all. I will try and get the dragon's blood back as well. Find Ellavorn and have him heal you."

Adasser nodded and started to climb the steps as another ball of black magic went flying towards him, striking him in the back and knocking him to the floor.

Arianna let out another scream, "Noooooooooooooo!"

She ran to him again and took him in her arms.

He looked up at her and ran his finger across her cheek.

"I am sorry, I should have listened to you. I have failed you."

Arianna began to shake and cry.

"No, Adasser, please, please don't leave me! I need you to finish training me. I can't do this without you. Please!"

Adasser shook his head, his breathing growing more shallow.

"Arianna, I am so proud to call you my granddaughter. I wish that we had had more time together. You are ready for this. You will win. I will not be able to be there to see it, but I will always be with you."

Tears were streaming freely down Arianna's face.

"No, please, stay. I've only just found you. Please don't leave. I love you."

Adasser smiled.

"I love you too." He took one last look at Arianna, closed his eyes and breathed his last breath.

Arianna let out a guttural scream and slid his body off of her. She stood and white magic flew in sparks from her fingertips. She turned and blew the wall in front of her to pieces, revealing nothing.

"You will pay for this! I will see to it!" She yelled into the darkness of the cells.

She blew another wall to rubble and another.

"Child, you must calm down. Your anger will not help you."

"Améthystos, I can handle this."

"No, calm your anger."

"No!" She blew another wall to rubble, and then another. The last wall came down and the rubble pile lay beneath a window, the sunlight streaming down on it. The Dark Figure laughed as it stepped from the shadows.

"Did I kill your precious grandfather?"

Arianna shot a ball of light at it without a word.

It jumped back, shocked that she would throw the first attack.

Arianna was seething with anger by now.

The Dark Figure was backing up, away from her, the fear it felt was coming in waves. Arianna threw another ball of light. She noticed that it had the dragon's blood in its hand. She threw another ball and hit the jar, shattering it. It was the Dark Figure's turn to scream.

"Oh, did I break your stupid jar? Too bad you won't be able to use it now."

The Dark Figure threw a ball of black magic at her and hit her shoulder, knocking her down to the ground.

The scene looked familiar from the dream that Arianna had had while at Magus's house. She threw another ball of white light just as Améthystos shot her ice encased fire into the room. The Dark Figure went to move to throw another ball of magic at her, but she was quicker. Her white energy flew past its head, catching the hood and knocking it off, revealing its face.

Arianna gasped at the familiar face as The Dark Figure sneered at her and then disappeared into a cloud of smoke.

To be concluded...

ACKNOWLEDGMENTS

I would love to thank my daughters: Abby and Cecilia. You two are my whole heart and the reason that I wake up every day. You've encouraged me along this ride and I hope that you can stick with me for at least another one more. I can't tell you enough how much I love you girls. You're my whole heart.

I want to thank my parents. Mom, Dad, who have always encouraged my interest in writing. You two are the absolute best parents a girl could ever hope for.

To my extended family: My brother, Bill, who is a pretty cool guy. Thank you for the votes of confidence when I needed them. Krista, I love you, girl! You deserve a medal for putting up with my brother. Mom-mom, without whom I would not have been able to get this book up and running so quickly. Granny, who gives me a role model to look up to every single day. Aunt Ceil, who I can always count on to give me an honest opinion on things.

For my "girl squad," especially Holly and Micki. You guys have stuck with me through the lowest of my lows and have loved me through it all, even when I wasn't so loveable. Chelsey, I know we met later, but thank you for sticking by me through so much in that time. I don't know what I would do without you girls.

To my editor, Amy, thank you! You are amazing! I am so glad Micki introduced us!

To my cover designer, Pierre, you made my vision even better than I imagined. The cover is truly stunning. Check him out on Fiverr (artbypierre.)

To my coworkers, Phanit, Kwadina, Tysha, Suzanne, Rebekah, and Lynn, you guys make the day so much more fun. Thank you for the daily laughs.

ABOUT THE AUTHOR

Chrissy White was born and raised in Philadelphia, PA, where she still lives with her two daughters. She has always had a love of reading. As a child, her mother would read "normal" children's stories to her brother and her, while her father would tell them stories from The Lord of the Rings, and other series like them. This inspired a love of fiction and fantasy that still prevails today. She has always loved to write, and has had several poems published by the National Library of Poetry. Throughout high school, she would entertain her friends with short stories. She enjoys baking, spending time at the beach, crafting, trying to paint, and being with her family.

www.ingramcontent.com/pod-product-compliance
Lightning Source LLC
Chambersburg PA
CBHW070158260626
47160CB00002B/376